BLACK DONALD

N. M. GILLSON

Black Donald is a work of fiction. Names, characters, places, and incidents either are the product of the author's imagination or are used fictitiously. Any resemblance to actual persons, living or dead, events, or locales is entirely coincidental.

N M Gillson has asserted his right under the Copyright Designs and Patents Act 1988 to be identified as the author of this work.

Black Donald is also available as an eBook.

Copyright 2011 N. M. Gillson
3rd Edition 2023
All rights reserved.
ISBN: 1466254513
ISBN-13: 978-1466254510

ACKNOWLEDGEMENTS

This is the 3rd edition of Black Donald, and hopefully the most improved. I want to thank everyone who has helped me along the way. Piotr, a fellow writer friend who encouraged me initially to write something outside my comfort zone. Paula, a fellow teacher and writer, who also read some of the earlier manuscripts, providing some encouragement and ideas. To my students who have discovered this book online and asked their parents to get it for them, you are truly wonderful, never change.

1

Kirkfale, Scotland
1910

"Rose, are ye in? Can I come in?" A tall, slender man with grey hair stood in the centre of the sandy road facing the shoe-maker's shop. He wore a long black cloak that trailed on the ground and was covered in dirt at the hem. The relentless rain had been falling for several days soaking his hair and ageing face, but it seemed not to affect him or his endeavours. His shoulders hung as if they were weary from having walked for days, but his arms were clasped before him as if to show respect for who he was talking to. He looked through the gap of the window now covered by a board to see if there was any sign of movement within the wooden building. Nothing.

In the distance, the overflowing rivers that usually flowed along the outskirts of the village of Kirkfale, crashed down the nearby mountains. The crackling sounds carried through the small, twisted streets and echoed off every structure in the ancient settlement, creating a rustling melody to the backdrop of rising mountains. A solitary bird on a desperate search for its next meal sliced through the heavy rain. Ignoring the dark, grey clouds that hovered above emptying their watery contents onto the ground below, it circled before landing on a rock outcrop covered in pale moss.

Nestled in the heart of the deepest valleys of the Grampian Mountain Range in Scotland, Kirkfale was largely unknown to outsiders. The main roads connecting the towns of the North to those of the South had been laid several miles south of the village. With one road in and out of Kirkfale, the villagers seldom left the valley and rarely accommodated guests who dared venture this far into the mountains. It came as a big surprise to many of the villagers, at first, when they discovered this stranger staying with the owner of the shirt shop a few months ago. As the days went on, his presence was more accepted allowing him to move between villagers, making use of their hospitality and learning their skills. Through the course of gossip, the stranger had been called many names, but one seemed to be favoured above all others, *Black Donald*.

"Come on, open up, I only wanna be your friend," Black Donald said with a cheery voice. Truth be known, he was struggling to hide his annoyance, he failed to understand why this one shop, the last one before the end of the village, had closed when all the others had accepted him with open arms. This last shop lay between him and his goal. That annoyed him. "I'll tell ye what, ye open your door and teach me ev'rythin' ye ken and I'll see to it that ye'll thrive and become rich beyond your wildest dreams." He smiled, but it soon dropped to a grimace. HOW DARE SHE RESIST ME.

Despite the rain, the street quickly filled up with villagers when they heard Black Donald's persistent shouting. They gathered on both sides talking to one another and wondering why Rose, the shoemaker, was not answering. After a few more minutes, Donald turned to the villagers and pleaded, "Does anybody ken where Rose is? She's no' answerin' her door." He wanted to smile at the gathered crowd, it had not taken him long to alter their perceptions and turn them to his will and desires. *It was easy; they are all weak-willed.* Instead, he looked pleadingly at those around him, but nobody made a move to help. Despite his 'power' over these people, they still showed signs of mistrust, *perhaps they are not as weak-willed as I thought.* Eventually, a small boy gingerly stepped forward. No higher than Black Donald's waist, he carried a basket in which Donald presumed he had bread, "What do ye ken, Son?" he said softly to the boy.

"Mister, Rose as awa' th'day. She said she'll no' be back for some time and if anybody asked where she was, I was to say that." The boy beamed at Donald with a grin from ear to ear.

Donald nodded his head, "What's yer name, Son?"

"Tommy, Mister." Donald was amazed Tommy showed no sign of fear or apprehension. He had recognised the boy, but the name placed him as the farmer's son, and he realised why he had so much confidence.

Taking a step closer, Donald contemplated his next move. "Are ye no' that bairn from the farm at the top o' the village?" Of course, he knew the answer, but manipulating the boy would get him the information he needed.

"Aye that I am, Mister." Tommy replied with pride. He puffed out his chest and stood as tall as he could as if a rod had been pushed down his shirt and trousers.

"Your father taught me how to gather wool from sheepies?"

"Aye that he did, Mister." Tommy nodded slightly. The corners of Donald's mouth began to curl slowly upwards.

"An' your mother taught me how to turn th'wool into a jumper?"

"Aye that she did, Mister," Tommy maintained his smug demeanour and did not take his eyes away from Black Donald. If he were anyone else, Black Donald would have found that disconcerting and uncomfortable, but he was beginning to like Tommy's charisma.

"Are ye sure you heard the message, right? Do ye have any idea where she's gone and when she'll be back?"

Tommy thought for a moment before answering, "I dinna ken all that, Mister, but I'm tellin' ye noo, Rose is no' there, she left the other day wi' big bags an' seemed in a hurry." He stretched his arms out to signify the size of the bags allowing the basket to sway a little.

"And ye are sure about that noo'?" He wanted to be sure, but he had discerned from Tommy that this endeavour was pointless. Rose, the only one who could teach him how to make shoes, was gone.

"Aye!" Black Donald nodded in defeat and sighed. He allowed his anger well up inside. His plan had been foiled again, like so many times before. This time, however, it would be different; he still controlled the moment.

Black Donald looked into Tommy's eyes, a small part of him was sad that he would have to do what he was about to do, but he refused to let something like human emotion get in his way. He looked up to the crowd behind Tommy, "Have I no' paid ye handsomely for all your hospitality? Have I no' been generous wi' ma wealth in return for your skills?" He threw his arms into the air, "Do ye think I canna hear ye, mutterin and laughin behind my back? What have I done to deserve your disloyalty? I could have gone anywhere to learn these skills, but I chose Kirkfale because I believed ye were a good people. Clearly, I was wrong!"

He slid his aged and haggard hand into the front opening of his robe and then retracted it slowly. As the hand left the robe, it clasped the hilt of a sword. Within seconds, he had withdrawn the long, thin blade and had raised it above his head with both hands. His robe lifted off the ground as his arms stretched up in readiness for Black Donald to make his first strike, his feet barely visible. The multi-faceted ruby at the end of the hilt reflected rays of red light over Donald's face creating an eerie glow. His eyes turned fiery amber, and his cheeks wrinkled deeper as he bared his teeth and began to snarl.

The villagers screamed and ran in every direction, bumping into each other but somehow, scrambling away. Some ran into their shops or houses and locked the doors the best they could. "Look at ye all run as if there are places to hide from my power." Donald's voice boomed throughout the valley like a lion's roar. The screech of a bird sounded high above his head, but he ignored it, "I'll find ye all. I'll slay ye all. Then I'll burn yer whole village down to the ground. Not one of ye will escape my wrath. Ye all will be damned to hell and the one who brought this upon ye, will perish; her and her descendants." He roared again. Several nearby windows smashed spraying frantic villagers with shards of glass.

Donald looked back at the boy, why had he not run like the others? He stood watching Donald, albeit drenched from the rain.

"Mister, why are your…" He began but stopped when fear struck his face for the first time since stepping forward from the crowd.

Black Donald swung his sword in one swift motion at Tommy slicing his midsection with little effort. He watched Tommy's face as his eyes went bloodshot and maroon blood appeared at his mouth, "Shame, I liked you." Without another thought, he turned and singled out his next victim.

2

Preston, England,
6 months ago

The reflected sunlight from the shop windows across Fishergate was dimmed through the tinted glass of the bank doors. Mary Cameron stood facing the doors, ignoring the slow-moving traffic outside; instead, looking at her image in the window. Her deep brown eyes told of the sadness she felt in her heart, a feeling that was confirmed by the tear that trickled its way down her right cheek. She combed her fringe of black hair over her left ear and wiped the tear away with the back of her hand.

Sniffing slightly, Mary hoped no one heard her and would ask if she was alright. She knew that would make her burst out crying. Mary wanted to scream but saw the security guard in the corner of her eye standing just to the left of the doors. Anything out of the ordinary would encourage him to move and intercept her.

A young lady and her child entered the bank and for a moment the noise from the street outside filled the entire room, but then died down when the door closed. Looking around, Mary realised why the waiting room was so quiet; there were only a few people. She turned to face the tellers behind inch-thick glass shield wondering what their life was like working in a bank, with all that money? No doubt they are rolling in it and have no need to ask for any help. Suddenly she became aware of someone standing behind her and turned too quickly losing her balance.

The security guard caught her just in time before she crashed into a leaflet stand, "You alright, Miss?"

She looked up, his grey moustache hung limply over his lip and his half-moon glasses appeared out of place on the bridge of his nose, "Thank you, I just turned a little too quickly." She grinned.

He smiled and nodded, "That's fine, Miss." He took his arms away, "Would you like a seat, Miss?"

For a moment, she was going to say yes, but thought better of it; she had to get out of the bank. She shook her head, "No, thank you, I'll be alright." She straightened her jumper and began walking slowly towards the door.

"Excuse me, Miss, have you dropped this?" He held up her purple document wallet. She hoped she would be leaving the bank with an agreement to a loan in that wallet, but she had been refused. She felt her throat thicken and tears pricked at her eyes but fought it back taking the wallet.

"Thank you; I won't get very far without that, now, will I?" She faked a laugh but was not sure if she had pulled it off since the guard did not even smile. Placing the wallet in her bag, she turned back towards the door and opened it.

Her shoulders hung low in disappointment as she meandered out onto Fishergate. The warmth of the sun surprised her a little, but that was the last thing on her mind. She tried to comprehend why the bank had refused her a loan again and what her options were now, *I can't come this far and be stopped at the last hurdle.* She understood the current economic crisis had put no end of pressure on banks, but she was an honest person, or at least she hoped she was. Her thoughts were interrupted by her phone ringing in her bag.

"Hiya, Babe!" She tried to sound positive but knew her husband would sense in the tone of her voice that things did not go the way she wanted it to go. She could never fool him; he always got the truth out of her.

"Hey Babe, you sound sad," the voice said.

"Yeah, he said no, apparently with our current account being in the overdraft on a regular basis, I am a liability when it comes to money."

"What? Does he not know I have a stable job, want me to give him a ring?" Mary smiled. She recalled Iain, her husband was unhappy at first with her idea of becoming a professional shoemaker. She heard his voice telling her it was a waste of time in today's society, but when she discovered shoemaking made her happy after taking several night classes on different subjects; she knew in her heart that she was meant to make shoes.

"No! I just need to think of something else, there are always possibilities," she said. "Besides, if it is meant to be, it WILL happen." There was a silence, "will you be home late?" She drastically wanted to change the topic before she started crying again. She really did not want complete strangers to stop and look at her strangely as they passed.

"Shouldn't be, the meeting was cancelled since the heads ill. Tell you what, I'll get a bottle of wine and a pizza, and we'll watch a film or something."

She smiled again, "Love you."

"Love you too, Babe. Better go, the bells just rang, see you later."

"Bye, bye." She pressed the off button and began putting the phone back in her bag, when it rang. She smiled thinking it was Iain again like he used to do when they were dating, just to say, 'I miss you' or 'I love you', but the caller ID was withheld. "Hello?"

"Is that Mary Cameron?" A deep voice spoke with precision and expert pronunciation. The voice was definitely not Iain's normal voice, but he could have disguised it.

"Who is this?" Mary began to smile, thinking it was a joke, "Is that you, Iain?" This was something else Iain would do, just to play a trick on her. Her finger was poised on the off button just as the caller spoke again.

"Are you looking for premises for a self-employed business in shoemaking?"

"Excuse me?" This is definitely a crank call; she pressed the off button. She could not believe her ears and began searching for Iain's number to demand an explanation.

The phone rang again. She hesitated before answering, "Hello?" She hoped it was not the same caller as before.

"Mary, please do not hang up, this is a legitimate call and offer I want to present you with, I only ask for a few minutes of your time and patience. I understand that you are looking to start a shoe-making business, I can help, please trust me, I only want to help you succeed and bring trade to my village." The caller sounded serious, but Mary was not fooled.

"I'm onto you, Iain James Cameron, wait until I see you tonight."

"I assure you, Mary, I am not your husband. Let's just say, I am someone who can help you with your current financial predicament. You see, I am always on the lookout for fresh ideas that will bring back forgotten skills and trades. I only want to encourage you to start your shoe-making business with no loans, no overhangs and no overpowering boss. You will be totally in charge of your shoe-making shop, the staff of your choice, the decoration of your choice, everything will be yours."

She was about to respond, but the voice spoke again, "And if you think this is too good to be true, please do not, there are no catches whatsoever. You will be given everything you need to start and succeed, and any help will be given to you upon your request."

"Assuming I went with this? And that is not very likely at this point, what's in it for you?"

There was a soft giggle, "I assure you, Mrs Cameron, you and your husband will be handsomely rewarded with a fully furnished house, a location for your business, and a job in our local school for your husband. The only thing that I want from our business deal is that you teach me your trade."

Mary looked around to see if she could spot any hidden cameras, "Of course, I am not looking for a decision just now, I expect you to discuss it with your husband." Mary gulped and began shuffling her feet, "Mary, I am so confident you will make a great success I am offering you this unbeatable opportunity, no strings attached." There was a momentary silence, "I look forward to your decision forthwith."

The line went dead. Her lingering thought was, how she was going to get Iain back for this prank.

3

Kirkfale, Scotland,
3 weeks ago

"I declare MARY'S SHOES open." Iain watched as his wife squeezed the over-sized, black-handled scissors to snip the red ribbon that had been draped in front of the glass doors to her brand-new shop. He was quite surprised how quickly she had managed to set everything up. He considered the time Mary told him about the call she had received more than five months ago. An offer with no obvious catch, or so the caller had said. Mary had been so excited and after speaking with him immediately rang the stranger back and made initial plans. Iain, however, was a little more sceptical and still believed there to be some hidden catch, but because he loved her, he chose to let it go, hoping he was wrong.

    Iain recalled the journey just before entering Kirkfale. The luscious mountains, picturesque rivers and waterfalls, created a location fit for gods. The village was located at the base of the valley, with an ancient and derelict wall built around it. The original gateway still stood, but was now more for decoration than purpose, simply a physical remembrance to the village's heritage. On the east of the village, beyond the wall, was the boarding school. With its numerous towers and wings built into the mountain face, it resembled a medieval castle rather than a high-achieving school. It was slightly elevated above the village, perhaps indicative of its perceived importance, Iain could not be sure. He had dated the construction back as far as the early 14th century, but he knew looks could be deceiving.

Looking around at the gathered villagers, most of whom he had already spoken to, Iain quickly discovered he had to concentrate really hard to understand, given their broad Scottish dialect. He liked how they were close-knit; everyone seemed to know everyone else, and they were caring enough to hold a street party for Mary's shop opening, or perhaps it was just an excuse for a party.

He smiled a little when he surveyed the high street, shops and businesses lining the single, winding street for about half a mile into the village. Beyond that, there was not much to account for. Kirkfale, it would seem, was home to just under one hundred people and approximately one quarter of them were children who attended the boarding school. Iain found it strange that such a reputable school, according to Ofsted, was situated in the mountains near one of the smallest villages he had ever visited. However, he pushed those thoughts to the back of his mind and chose, rather to concentrate on other things, like Mrs. Doherty's cream and jam scones.

Tucking into his fourth scone, Iain recalled how it was only 6 months ago he had first heard of Kirkfale. Even the so-called prestigious boarding school, classed as one of the top in the UK, was new to him. He glanced over towards the school, but, as he expected, could not see it for trees and buildings of the village.

He put the last bit of the scone into his mouth and looked around the street. He saw villagers meandering in MARY'S SHOP looking at the old photos that were left in the building for the big opening day. Mary had felt obliged to display them along with some shoe designs she had already created before arriving. She was talking to someone outside her shop and was smiling and laughing a lot. Iain wondered if they would in fact, be happy in this small, forgotten village in the heart of Scotland.

Farmer Gallagher, his wife, Amanda, and their son, Thomas, were standing near a green tractor with a sign posted just to the left offering tractor rides to the children. There was a queue of children looking very excited. Next to them was a face painting stand, again with a line of children waiting patiently. Mr and Mrs Doherty were next with their cream and jam scones. Then the local policeman stood almost to attention, if it were not for the cup of beverage in his hand. Iain had not been able to speak with him yet and so made a mental note to introduce himself later when the party had died down. He looked at the policemen over the rim of his teacup, pretending to savour the taste of Mrs Danderson's delicious tea. He stood taller than Iain with a clean-shaven face and cropped hair. His helmet lay on the ground next to him. His uniform seemed in pristine condition making Iain wonder if it had pressed that very morning. Iain noticed the officer was looking straight at him, as if he were staring right into his soul. A shiver shot down his back and he looked back down.

Old Mr and Mrs Danderson sat on chairs outside their shop, *COATS, CLOAKS AND ROBES*, which was next to Mary's. Mr Danderson was sat behind a table with numerous paper cups, two tea pots and a coffee pot. It seemed at first glance he was snoozing with a newspaper atop his chest like a blanket, but then would move when someone came to the table, so he could pour a beverage and hand it to Mrs Danderson who gave it with a smile.

"You must be that new teacher starting up at the school?" A broad Scottish voice slightly startled Iain, forcing him to spill his tea, "Och! Sorry about that, Laddie, here, let me help you." Iain watched as the grey-haired lady took out a handkerchief and began wiping his shirt where the tea had spilt. It reminded him of his own dear sweet mother, who had died a few years before he got married. "So, are ye that lad?" The woman smiled her sweet smile, a sparkle flashed in her blue eyes, or perhaps it was a reflection in her horn-rimmed glasses.

"Yes, I am Iain, I start on Monday." He was excited, knowing he was about to start a job where his experience mattered. He was looking forward to the occasional night-time supervision of the school and starting up a fencing club for the senior boys and girls. He ran through all the plans he had made in his head and smiled. This would be the first in his career where he had free rein to do as he liked without worry for lack of resources or school funds. A school like the Kirkfale Grammar was a school of prestige and was well off. Students who attended, according to the school's website, came from all over Scotland and paid a handsome amount of money for the privilege.

"Looking forward to it then? Bet ye are, tis a grand school, one of the best in Scotland, no doubt. The headmaster is one of the best in country and because of all the hard work he has done with our kids, the villagers elected him Mayor of Kirkfale. I'm telling you now, that was the best decision we made, because he has done everything to get Kirkfale noticed by the rest of Scotland. You may have noticed, there is only one road into and out of Kirkfale because of the landscape, that is a major disadvantage when trying to conduct business around the country. The mayor has done a fine job already and we have a steady stream of tourists coming on a regular basis to Kirkfale." She was about to say something else, before Iain gently placed his hands on her shoulders and smiled.

"I'm sorry, Mrs…?" He suddenly realised that he did not know this woman and hoped that she would not scream for him touching her shoulders. He glanced at the policeman.

"Mrs Crochet, Laddie," she said sweetly.

"I'm sorry, Mrs Crochet, I think Mary needs me, however, I would love to hear more about the school and the village another time, perhaps." He tried to let her down gently but was not sure if he had achieved it.

"Och aye! That's my shop down there; you're more than welcome anytime." She pointed to the building just a few yards down on the opposite side of the road, "the post office, that is," she said to confirm.

"Well, when I am next passing, I'll pop in and share a cup of tea with you." He smiled and walked away towards Mary who was standing talking to another villager. Stopping next to her, he waited for her friend to leave before speaking, "So, you happy?" Iain took hold of Mary's arm and kissed her gently on the cheek.

"Are you kidding? I'm loving this!" She turned and wrapped her arms around Iain and kissed him on the lips, "Thank you, for agreeing to come."

"Hey, I needed a new challenge, I was going nowhere in that last school," he lied and hoped Mary did not notice. "This change will do us both good." He smiled before looking at the villagers and tried to listen to the bustle that filled the high street. Everything was rolling into one loud noise, making it impossible to hear any one conversation.

Finally, his eyes fell upon the table of scones, "Here, you have got to try one of these scones, they are absolutely delicious." He took a plate carrying a scone covered in cream and jam and gave it to Mary, "Seriously, you have not tasted anything as gorgeous as these." He helped himself to another from the table.

"I noticed you liked them; I've seen the five you've scoffed." She smiled taking the plate and began breaking a piece off. Iain loved that about her; she always did that with cakes and as a result, rarely made any crumbs. He, however, took a large mouthful irrespective of the outcome.

"Four actually, this is my fifth," he said after swallowing the mouthful.

Iain spotted the policeman again, this time standing on the opposite side of the road. His tall physique made him stand at least a head's length above everyone else. Iain felt another shiver shoot down his back and leaned over to Mary, "Hey, what do you make of him?" nodding in the policeman's direction.

Mary looked across the road, "Who?"

"The polic…" He looked back, but the officer was gone. Iain took a few steps, looked up and down the road, but could not see him. Returning back to Mary he shook his head, "That's odd, I could have sworn the policeman was watching me."

"It was probably just your imagination, too many scones," she said poking his belly, "nothing to worry about. Come on, this is supposed to be a party, ain't it?"

Mary kissed him on the nose and walked into her shop to mingle with some potential customers. Iain smiled and nodded but continued looking.

4

Present Day

"Hey Buddy, all ready for tonight?" Iain ignored the excited chant as it punched through the sombre atmosphere of the staffroom. The rain tapped on the ancient stained-glass windows in a chaotic symphony as a small group of teachers sat discussing children and their associated behavioural incidences. Iain had wondered why it was always the disruptive children and not the good ones that were talked about. The music teacher snorted, startling himself from his slumber in the corner armchair. Wriggling his nose, he sniffed as he combed his hand through his long greying beard. A loud rustling newspaper caught Iain's attention, and although he could not see the reader, he guessed he was demanding quietness. He caught sight of the newspaper headline and suddenly felt an immense sadness as the comprehension of what he read sunk in. A thought went to the families of the 50 school children who drowned when a river burst its banks. He closed his eyes wondering when the rain would stop, just as he felt a nudge on his arm.

"Hey, are you ignoring me or something?" He opened his eyes and, although a little startled, smiled. The new arrival beamed a large grin back showing his brilliantly bright, white teeth that looked more at home in Hollywood than Kirkfale. His ginger hair hung past his shoulders and together with his boyish facial features, they gave him a look of youth, an image Iain often yearned for as he approached his fourth decade.

"Sorry, Andy..." Iain spluttered, his mind still conjuring up images of the 50 children drowning.

"Hey, you alright, you're looking a bit peaky." Iain was glad that his friend Andrew was a fellow Englishman with an accent he could easily understand without having to concentrate too hard, although, he was getting used to the Scottish accent more these days.

"Do I?" He could not think of anything else to say, "Perhaps I'm coming down with something." He instinctively felt his forehead for heat but found nothing out of the ordinary.

"Tell you what, I'll do your duty tonight and you go home to your lovely wife and get some rest," he ordered. "Clearly you are still adjusting to the new climate."

Iain sniggered, "What, perpetual rain?"

"Hey, we do get some sunshine, you know." Andrew said in a mocking tone before smiling.

"Oh yeah, I remember, one day a year, blink and you'll miss it." They both burst out laughing, ignoring the loud rustle and 'tut' from the teacher holding the newspaper.

"That's better; at least there is some colour in your cheeks now." Andrew nudged Iain's arm again, "So, you all prepared for your rounds?"

"I think so, not much to prepare for though, really," Iain said nodding.

"Just be on your guard for the Ghost of Wallace House."

"What?" Iain eyed his friend, trying to ascertain whether he was being serious or not, after all, he had not heard anything about this before.

"Yeah, the ghosts of past headmasters are said to roam Wallace House. Did you know that was the original location of the headmaster's office? Apparently, as the stories go, several of the past headmasters committed suicide over stress and as a result are forced to roam the corridors of what is now Wallace House." Andrew looked down to overt eye contact with Iain.

"Shut up, you Muppet! I'm not THAT daft!" Iain smiled and gently punched Andrew on the shoulder when he burst out laughing, eliciting another newspaper rustle. "What you up to tonight?"

"Got fencing practice down at the club," Andrew said, "you know you should come next week." Iain was seriously tempted. He had been a keen fencer back in Preston, having won several competitions over the years. Although, he had only taken up the hobby in the last decade, he had developed a strong love for the sport and as such, had progressed quickly up the ranks, but reluctantly gave it up after he and Mary got married.

"I might just take you up on that offer," he said, although he knew Mary would never allow him to. She was adamant it was too dangerous a sport that could cause extreme harm, despite his explanations of the safety equipment and protocols involved. It had eventually come down to whether he loved fencing more than his gorgeous wife. To Iain, there was no competition.

*

Iain felt a shiver shoot down his back as he turned the corner making the spot of white light from the torch dance around the dark corridor. Although he knew ghosts did not exist, the story Andrew told him earlier in the staffroom played havoc on his subconscious. He understood the need to turn off the corridor lights to simulate night within the school, but it still felt too much of an ask for night supervisors to walk around just with a torch. He had narrowly missed several statues already by walking too close to the corridor walls or turning a blind corner. He was sure he had missed checking a number of locked doors as well, just because he had not seen them as the beam of light was concentrated on his path. He decided he would have to bring the topic up at the next staff meeting, requesting dim lighting along the corridors, at least until the rounds were completed.

It was some comfort, however, that he was only expected to explore the corridors once during the night. He did not mind staying in the Wallace House common room for the rest of the time; he could simply just sit in one of the comfy armchairs and snooze until morning. Having checked most of the classrooms on route, he was satisfied no children were roaming the school without permission and his final check would be to confirm they were all tucked up in bed, fast asleep.

He turned into another corridor and gave out a sigh of relief when he realised the only exit lead straight to the common room, however, as he approached, he noticed a slim line of light escaping round the edge of the badly fitted wooden door. As he padded closer, his first instinct was to burst in and scare whoever was in the room out of their skins. He recalled using a similar tactic on new year-7 classes in previous jobs, to ensure his authority was secure in their minds. However, he stopped just outside the door and listened as dull voices penetrated the wood.

He could only make out the odd word, but not enough to make sense of it and so placed his hand on the handle ready to push it open. He knew the old door squeaked, like most doors in the school, but he figured he would be able to open to door before anyone scampered up the stairs to the sleeping quarters. He was about to push when the light went out.

Wondering if they had heard him, he instinctively moved his hand away from the door. Moments later, he heard a scraping sound but had no idea what would have caused it. Gently pushing the door, he jumped as it gave out a squeal at the hinges.

The common room was empty.

He listened out for soft thuds on the wooden steps to the sleeping quarters, but heard none, and although he knew that was not a definitive answer, he was satisfied with it. Instead, a clunk grabbed his attention, and he snapped around to the fireplace, though at first glance, the source was nowhere to be found. Kneeling down to see if he could find anything that would explain the sound, he found nothing. "You're losing it, Iain," he said sitting on the hearth.

He rested his head against the stone fire-surround and allowed the stone's coolness to sooth his back muscles, whilst he looked around the room. Heaving out a large breath, he conceded that he had heard nothing earlier, and the light was merely a trick caused by the reflection from his torch. It seemed he had been hearing things; *perhaps there were ghosts in Wallace House.* He smirked.

He slowly allowed his eyes to close, although he knew the consequences of poor circulation to his legs and bottom when he awoke, the soothing sensation of the stone hearth felt comfortable and eased him swiftly into a deep sleep.

Iain awoke to find himself walking the corridors at a hurried pace, and although he did not understand what was going on, initially, he continued walking. He looked over his shoulder just as he turned a corner and was glad nothing was following but missed that something was in front of him and stumbled backwards when he caught sight of his assailant. His heart began beating faster and harder, almost as if it were trying to escape his chest to flee the apparition before him.

From the oak floor, Iain watched as the ghostly figure glided forward. Although it was distinctly white, to Iain it resembled mist in the early morning slowly moving over the mountains around Kirkfale. As it crept closer, Iain spotted the dark piercing eyes that looked directly at him, wanting to penetrate his very soul. That alone was enough to scare him half to death, but to make matters worse, he could not move.

He tried to stand, but somehow, the apparition held him in a trance. He was captivated by the trenchant eyes of the ethereal figure and lost all sensation in every muscle of his entire body. All he could do was wait for the ghost to engulf him and do whatever a ghost did. Just as all hope seemed lost, he heard several dull voices from behind…

Opening his eyes to the welcomed sight of the darkened common room, he realised he had fallen asleep. Moving his right leg, he immediately seized it with both hands as pin pricks shot all along it. His first instinct was to cry out in pain but clenched his teeth and eyes instead. Gritting his teeth through the pain, he forced himself to stand, hoping the blood would return quicker. However, before he reached the chair, he heard a scraping sound from behind him. Quickly twisting his head toward the fire, Iain held back a gasp as he witnessed the large surround sliding to the right, apparently with no external help.

He darted behind the sofa and crouched down. Holding his breath, he hoped he had not been spotted or heard. He peered round the side of the sofa, ensuring he was still well hidden in the shadows and watched as two senior boys appeared from behind the fire, or at least where the fire had been and headed up towards the dormitory.

Iain listened to the decreasing echo of their footsteps. Only when he had heard the door of their sleeping quarters squeal open and slam shut did he crawl out from behind the sofa. He struggled to understand what he had just witnessed as the fireplace returned to its resting place just as Iain reached it. Running his hands over the darkened grooves of the fireplace, he searched for some switch that controlled the fire. There was no such switch. He rested his right hand on the mantelpiece and inadvertently nudged the candlestick on display. He tutted at his lack of thinking and shook his head. The candlestick slid effortlessly to the side and within seconds the fire began moving with the scraping, he kept looking over his shoulder for signs of life. When the fire disappeared, the back wall opened up to reveal a dimly lit tunnel leading to a stone stairwell. Despite his nerves exploding in trepidation, his historical interest enticed him to proceed.

Steadily, Iain descended the dusty steps and shook his head, the whole idea of secret passages in an ancient building was a complete cliché and it was all he could do to stop laughing. At the bottom of the stairs, he continued along another dimly lit corridor. The occasional fire-torch hung from both walls and was covered in white, stringy cobwebs. The ground was dusty and with every step, Iain sent up a small plume of dust and sand, which quickly settled back into place.

A few metres along the corridor, he began hearing faint voices up ahead. Picking up the pace, he reached a small wooden door that had been left ajar, no doubt by the boys who had been down there moments before. He peered through the thin gap between the door and its post but could see nothing, so he pushed. He scrunched his face hoping the door would not creak. When the door remained silent, he let out a small sigh, and continued to push. However, he did not want to push his luck too far and held back from swinging the door fully open.

5

Iain snuck through the gap but snagged his belt buckle as he passed the door. Looking down, he saw a large splinter of wood sticking out, nothing a gentle tug won't solve. He took hold of the metal buckle and pulled, hoping he would not make any sound, the last thing he wanted was to alert anyone to his presence at least until he had discovered what those boys had been doing beneath the school. The buckle came free with a small clink. He froze and listened for movement. When he was satisfied it was safe to proceed, he tiptoed forward. Although he could not make out what was being said, the presence of voices steered him in the right direction. He found a large stone boulder, hid behind it, and peered over it to get a better look.

Ignoring the coldness of the rock beneath his hands, Iain took a mental picture of the chamber just a few metres away. He guessed it was about 15 square metres with the ceiling about two metres above his head. Torches hung around the walls allowing the shiny rock that lined the walls and floor to reflect the light back into the chamber. Iain was unsure whether that was deliberate or not, but he had to agree it was an efficient use of resources. He could not imagine how long it had taken someone to chisel the chamber out of solid rock and wondered if the head even knew about the underground corridors and chamber.

There was a stone table standing on a small dais to the side of the chamber. Iain wondered if the dais was designed to create a focal point in the room, a hypothesis confirmed when hooded figures stood facing the table. All except one who stood on the dais and looked out onto the others.

Each of the hooded figures wore a black robe; so long they trailed on the floor. Those that stood facing the one, who, Iain presumed, was the leader, had their hands clasped in front of them and bowed their heads slightly. He could hear a low-level mutter, barely audible. The leader held his hands and his face up towards the roof, as if he were saying a prayer. Despite straining to see, Iain could not see the figure's face. The inside of his hood, dark.

After a few minutes, the 'prayer' had ended, and the leader lowered his hands placing one into his robe. From behind him, two hooded figures appeared guiding a small boy. The boy wore a red robe with a yellow trim which extended just shy of the granite floor. Iain recognised the boy, but he could not put a name to his face. He watched as he was lowered to his knees and forced to bow his head. The leader placed his free hand on the boy's head and chanted once again and as he did so, he caressed the boy's scalp gently. Seconds later, he took his hidden hand out of his robe and to Iain's horror, wielded a dagger and immediately thrust it into the boy's neck. Blood squirted out over the dais and the boy's cloak.

"What the hell are you doing?" Iain could not contain his shock or anger. With the echo of his voice still ringing in the chamber, he clambered through the flustering followers heading straight for the kneeling, now swaying and clutching his neck. His lips were moving, but Iain could only see watery glugs that reminded him of bubbles bursting at the surface of water. Blood ooze between his fingers, forming a puddle at his knees.

"You dare interrupt the sacred ritual of first blood?" shouted one of the followers stepping in to block Iain, but he pushed the hooded figure away.

"I'll damn-well interrupt anything that brings harm to a child," he reached down to the fallen boy and checked the wound before turning to the leader, now leaning over Iain. He instinctively applied pressure to the wound with his hand, hoping it would be enough, whilst maintaining focus on the one standing just in front of him holding the dagger. He heard scuffles and yells from behind. Most had already scarpered off like spiders when light is shone on them. Even as he knelt there holding the boy's bleeding neck, he could feel the life draining from him. That, and the hooded figure holding a dagger, he was out of options.

"You don't know what you are doing, old man," a youthful voice called, though Iain could not identify which hooded figure had said it. Iain weighted up the threat. Could he survive the odds of four against him and still help the child survive? Would Mary become a widow so quickly after moving up to Kirkfale? The figure took a small step closer.

Knowing shouting was not going to get him anywhere, Iain decided to take a softer approach and calmed his voice, "Look, what you have done here; do you even understand what the ramifications are for killing someone? Don't you realise what consequences come with taking a life?"

"You think you can come down here and make demands? Wait until the Master hears of this," said another, a Yorkshire accent.

"It is you who is sticking your nose in where it has no business being," said another, this one Scottish.

"Stay where you are, all of you!" With his free hand, he reached into his pocket and pulled out his mobile, "I am calling an ambulance and informing the police of this disgusting display of barbaric cowardice." Iain glanced down at the boy lying on the floor. His face turning paler with each wasted second.

"Get a grip old man, you are outnumbered four to one, you have no chance against us, or had you forgotten that we are the ones holding the weapon." Iain looked at the dagger being pointed at him, "So unless you want me to run you in myself, I would just forget what you saw here."

"Forget? You stabbed a boy, and unless he gets urgent medical care, he will die," he pointed towards the boy lying motionless on the floor, "I demand you let me get him to a hospital, NOW!" Rage surged through his veins and his head began throbbing with immense pressure as if it were about to erupt.

The leader moved the dagger closer to Iain's neck. A flash of light reflected off the blade, allowing Iain to see the figure snigger in derision. "You are in no position to demand anything, but I, however, am in the position to grant nothing." Iain felt the sharp tip of the dagger put pressure on his skin and he swallowed. "You trespass in the master's sacred temple and spout out demands, who do you think you are…God's angel?" Sheer contempt oozed from every spat-out word. Iain realised his tormentor was, however, just a boy and perhaps one he had taught. "Now, you are going to return to where you came from and forget all about what you have seen here."

Iain felt the dagger apply a little more pressure, "or I will see to it, you never talk again." He felt the rank breath of the teenage boy standing before and wanted to vomit but fought it back. "Do you understand, Old Man?"

"Joseph Roberts? Is that you?" asked Iain. The figure said nothing, "Come on guys, do you seriously think you are going to get away with this?" He was mentally preparing himself to thrust the dagger out of the boy's hand but kept his eyes on the shadow that filled his hood. "Killing someone changes you, it will start playing on your mind and before you realise it, you are stuck in a…" Iain did not finish his sentence. He felt his body lifted up and then forcibly smashed into the cold, hard rock floor. Blood began to pool to the side of his head. He tried to fight the dizziness but could only watch helplessly as a fifth figure allowed the four hooded murderers to escape, before retreating himself.

6

Light flooded into Iain's retinas and half blinded him as he opened his eyes. He shut them quickly. When he was ready, he slowly reopened them again and although the echoes of light remained, it was not as intense as the real thing. He looked round the room to see where he was, but a shooting pain shot through his skull forcing him to screw his eyes and grab the side of his head. It was then he realised the comfortable sensation of the bed mattress beneath him and wondered how he had got there. He recognised the curtains surrounding him as those from the hospital wing, and on the cabinet next to his bed was a large vase of yellow flowers. He could not recall what type, but they provided colour to the rather bland white walls. Next to the vase was a clear jug of water and a half-filled glass; a sudden urge to drink came upon him. He reached out and grabbed the glass. Another pain shot through his head as if a sledgehammer was being haphazardly thrown around inside his skull, but he ignored it and sipped the water. The water was surprisingly fresh and cool. He felt the coldness coat his lungs and chest revitalising him and re-energising his muscles and mind.

When he began to feel more like himself, he wondered how long he had been in the hospital wing and what had happened to those boys. Of course, he only knew for certain two of them were boys, but he could guess the others were of similar age. He would have to inform the headmaster. Deciding he had to do something, he threw the covers off and swung his legs over to the side of the bed; an alarm sounded. Two figures dressed in medicinal whites appeared instantly and began to fuss over him.

"Ah! Mr. Cameron you're back in the land of living. You don't want to rush out of bed so soon, however, you have suffered a nasty bash on your head,"

"Yes, I know," he said whilst subconsciously rubbing his temple, "some boy hit me from behind." He did not want to give too much information; in case she began asking questions he could not answer. He had to get to the Head immediately, before any other boys were killed. He had to get the police involved.

"Mr. Cameron, I must insist you return to bed, you're not fit to walk just yet. You may be sufferin' concussion." The woman turned to her burly companion and gave a silent command. He obeyed without word.

He stepped forward and began lifting Iain's legs back onto the bed. His hands felt rough, as if he had worked in an industrial job in the not-too-distant past. As he bent low, the light from the ceiling reflected off the nurse's bald head and Iain caught glimpse of a woman's head tattooed on his nape, with a body extending well below his shirt collar, though Iain could only guess as much. As the nurse stood, Iain spotted the sparkling crystal stud in his right ear.

When the covers were replaced over Iain, the large nurse tucked the edges under the mattress.

"Just out of interest, did they catch the boy who attacked me?" Iain wanted to fish for more information, but chances were the medical staff did not know much about the hidden underground chamber.

"I don't think you understand completely, Mr. Cameron. You were found by one of the Wallace House prefects at the bottom of the stairs leading up to the common room. He wasn't sure how long you'd been there, but he and a friend brought you here immediately." The female nurse looked at the chart at the end of the bed, "You were quite lucky they found you when they did, otherwise you would be in a far worse situation."

"But…" he tried to argue but could not think of the words. Everything was hazy in his mind and although he knew there was a hidden chamber where he was attacked, he could not be sure if it was indeed true and not something he had imagined. He was finding it hard to think straight with such a painful headache. "I'm sure I was attacked."

The nurse replaced the clip board on the end of the bed and clicked her pen into her tunic pocket, before turning to the male nurse, "Give Mr. Cameron another dose of sedatives, 20ccs." The nurse nodded.

"Aye." He turned, flicked the curtains open and disappeared.

"Look," Iain said wanting to sound authoritative, "there is a boy, I don't know his name, and he's dying…or dead on the floor of a chamber hidden below this school. You need to go find him before it is too late, Nurse, and we have to call the police, immediately." The woman smiled and stepped closer to Iain.

"First of all, I'm not a nurse, I'm Doctor Crivvens and second of all, I've been in this school for well over 15 years and I haven't found any hidden chambers anywhere in the school." She smirked, "Besides, do you not think that is a cliché?"

Iain realised he was not going to get anywhere and so nodded and faked a smile hoping it was believable, "Yeah, I guess I suffered a harder knock than I thought." He tapped his finger to the side of his head and laughed. The pain had subsided somewhat, but no one would believe him now.

The muscle-bound nurse returned with a metal kidney dish that rattled as the syringe rolled from side to side, "Raigmore are ready for transfer, Doctor, they have a bed cleared for Mr. Cameron." His voice was deep and emotionless. Iain wondered how he managed to become a nurse, but then reasoned that could be why he worked in a school. The doctor took the bed pan and looked at Iain. Iain assumed Raigmore was another hospital, but not sure where.

"Mr. Cameron, I really think you need some more rest, this sedative will help you relax more." She took the needle out of the kidney dish and checked it had no air bubbles in it by pressing the syringe plunger just enough to squirt a little clear liquid from the needle.

"No please, there is no need. I'm sorry; I will stay here and be a good boy." He smiled, "Besides I want to see my wife when she arrives." He tried to back off from the doctor, even though he knew he could not go far.

"Aye, I understand, but you have missed her already, she was here earlier on during visiting hours." Doctor Crivvens smiled a broad grin and took hold of Iain's arm and began tapping for a blood vessel.

Iain widened his eyes, "How long have I been here?"

"You were brought in yesterday morning with a severe laceration to your head. You had been on the floor all night." She smiled and held up the sedative, "Now, am I going to have to use this thing?"

Iain shook his head, "I think I can sleep without it, thanks. The pain is not as intense as it was." The doctor focused her eyes upon Iain's for a moment as if to read his mind and then nodded.

"Ok. Try to rest and remember this sedative is always available if you struggle. I've cleared it with the headmaster that you be given sick leave for a week to fully recover. I'll inform Raigmore that the bed is no longer needed. You should be able to go home tomorrow to rest." She smiled, placed the needle back in the kidney dish and walked out with the nurse following her.

Iain sighed. He hated needles, although, he did enjoy the prospect of being sent home the next day and spending a week without children to teach. However, he had to speak to the headmaster and tell him what he knew, even if it was all his imagination. That being said, it had felt so real, he was not convinced that it had been anything but reality. He rested his head onto his pillow with one thought flooding his mind; why had Mary not stayed until he awoke?

7

Another day slowly passed, "So, how you are feeling this morning, Mr. Cameron?" The doctor said as she opened the curtains and stepped inside his little cubical. "It's a fine day to spend at home; I wish I was so lucky." She smiled as she took his pulse, her eyes flicking back and forth between her pressing fingers and her small nurse's watch.

"I'm feeling a lot better and am able to move both legs with ease." He returned the smile.

"And the headaches?" she prompted whilst moving her inspection to his eyes.

"Gone," was all he said. Just as well, since the doors burst open allowing Mary to walk in with his coat and some presents and cards, "Ah, it looks like my ride has arrived." He nodded towards the door and beamed at Mary as she approached his bedside.

"Hey Babe, how you feeling?" She bent down and kissed him on the cheek, before turning to the doctor, "Is he free to go?"

"I can clear him for discharge, but he must rest at least until the end of the week." She turned to Iain, "You take it easy now, and come and see me next week." She smiled again and left the cubical.

"What's all this?" Iain asked as he moved his legs from the bed, thankfully, the nurse had untucked the sheet from beneath the mattress, so getting out of bed was relatively easy.

"One of the prefects of Wallace House stopped me when I arrived and gave them to me for you; they are from everyone in Wallace house. Ain't that sweet?" She smiled again.

"Yeah, they are great kids."

Mr Black phoned me earlier and shared his concerns about you. He mentioned that he had visited you once or twice but both times you were sleeping, and he felt he should not disturb you given your current health."

"That was nice of him," Iain was not convinced the headmaster had visited at all.

"Iain, you should be less cynical about your employer, he did provide for us."

Iain only grunted under his breath as Mary helped him put on his coat.

*

Iain could not remember the last time he felt so tired from walking, he was exhausted, and he had only walked from the hospital wing down one flight of stairs. A thought went to his classes that day and wondered if they had managed to get supply to cover at such short notice and if work had been set. He felt the urge to rush to his classroom to check all the work was in place and the students were behaving as he would expect if he were teaching them but knew Mary would refuse. Not only that, but he also had little strength to resist his wife's hand that held firm to his left forearm.

"Mr. Cameron, sir, you're up, that is great, when are you going to be teaching us again?" A young voice from behind called, enticing both Mary and Iain to turn and see who it was. Iain immediately smiled.

"George, it's *you*, not being a nuisance today for your supply, are you?"

"Me?" He pretended to be innocent before turning and running off in the opposite direction. Mary began to guide Iain back the way they were going, but Iain froze, his stance was firm. She pulled again, but to no avail. Iain was not going to budge, despite his weakened state; his strength was considerably more than Mary's. Defeated, she turned to look where he was looking.

"What's the matter?" Iain could sense worry in her voice.

"That boy, there, that boy he was…" He broke off as the boy came closer. Iain grabbed Mary's arm tighter and whispered, "That's him."

"What about him?" she asked.

"That small boy was the one who was killed in the downstairs chamber."

"Not that again! Doctor Crivvens mentioned you had been hallucinating." Iain stood firm as Mary tried to move him again. "The sooner we get you home, the better, where you can just rest and relax without the worry of work and students.

"I am not hallucinating, he really was there, but I saw him get stabbed, blood oozed out of him, and he lay there on the cold stone slab." The memory pained him, but he had to make Mary, of all people, believe him.

"Well, clearly he's not dead, which surely should tell you something is wrong with your tale." She gently nudged him around and guided him towards the main foyer where the main entrance was.

For the first time since awakening in the hospital wing, Iain was confused. "Come on, Sweetheart; let's get you home, where you can get away from all this."

As they moved closer to the foyer, a voice called from behind, "I hope you feel better soon, Sir." Iain recognised the voice, "Don't worry, Sir, I will make sure all your work is covered, just as you like it. You can count on me."

Without turning, he knew the owner of the voice was smirking. That voice was unmistakable. The last thing he wanted was to see the gloating face of his attacker.

8

"Are you sure you have everything you need, Babe?" Mary called from the hallway. Iain could just hear her through the closed lounge door. He knew she felt sad having to leave him like this, but equally, Iain knew she had to return to the shop. The pains of self-employment meant if you did not work, you did not get paid, so, he had agreed to let her go.

He smiled at the memories of Mary mollycoddling him when he had been ill in the past, to the extreme of her preventing him from doing *anything* for himself. To that end, he was a little relieved when Mary had told him she needed to get back to the shop. He had some things to think about.

"I'm fine; you go and tend to your customers." He knew that despite the closed door, she would be looking in his direction, probably reconsidering her decision about leaving him on his own. But the front door closed leaving Iain to bask in the quietness. He let out a sigh of relief when he heard the car engine start and fade as Mary drove off.

Within seconds, Iain began considering how to proceed about what he had witnessed at the school, but his thoughts were interrupted by the phone ringing. He contemplated letting it run into the voicemail but decided otherwise. He walked over to the side cabinet where he had flung his mobile earlier. His eyes glimpsed the caller ID as he pressed the connect button, "Hello Dad, you're back then." The sadness in his voice was obvious.

"Yeah, we got back about an hour ago." In comparison to his own voice, his father's sounded cheery which made Iain even more depressed.

"*We?*" Stressed Iain, knowing full well that he meant her! His so-called stepmother! But it was too late; Iain had blurted it out without thinking ahead. His mother had died 4 years ago, and Iain had been shocked when not even two months later, his father had turned up at the house one evening with Lainie and announced they were engaged. Lainie was slim and athletic with blonde hair that hung just below her shoulders. Her black-rimmed glasses accentuated her intellectual features and bright blue eyes. By all accounts, Lainie was a very attractive woman who, under different circumstances, would have been the object of Iain's affection, but there was something Iain did not understand; how did his father find someone so attractive so quickly and have such a loving relationship?

Over the years, Iain had convinced himself, that his father had been having an affair before his mother had died but had not the courage to confront him about it. Instead, he had developed a mistrust and disdain for his father so much so, they had become estranged from each other. Having moved from his father in Nottingham to live in Preston and now Scotland, had done nothing to help the situation.

"Yeah, Lainie and I, flipping long journey, Lainie is sleeping at the moment, the flight took it out of her."

Iain was not the least bothered about what Lainie was doing.

"So, Son, what have you been up to, how's that gorgeous wife of yours and is there any news of the patter of little feet in your household?" It was clear his father was trying to forget the past few years of estrangement, but then again, he had been in Australia on holiday for a long time.

"No children, MARY," he emphasised her name to point out he disapproved of his father calling her 'gorgeous', "is fine, thank you." He wanted to get away with saying a little as possible. He had things to do, important things.

"I just read your email about moving to Scotland…"

Iain sensed there was more to come by the tone of his father's words, but chose to interrupt, "Yes, we had to move for Mary's work."

"Mary's working now? Excellent, what's she doing?" His father sounded genuinely excited about it. Iain felt a little pleased but believed it was unlikely to be a truthful sentiment.

"She owns a shoe-making shop." His father burst out laughing.

"Are you serious? Who makes shoes these days?" Iain's small hope burst into a million pieces. He silently chastised himself for having a hint of hope.

"Mary does, she's quite good at it actually and it makes her happy. Besides, the village Mayor invited her to set up shop, giving her everything she needed to succeed."

"Sorry, Son, I meant no disrespect, if Mary is happy doing it, then good luck to her." Iain wanted to scream down the phone, but something inside him stopped him. "So where exactly in Scotland are you?

Your email was rather vague." Iain felt a surge of mistrust well up inside but forced it back.

"Kirkfale," he said.

His father fell silent for a moment before continuing, "No, really, where are you living?"

"I'm telling you; we live in Kirkfale. It's a village slap-bang in the middle of the valleys of the Grampian mountains."

"I know where Kirkfale was. I mean, I know I have been out of the picture for a while, but you should still remember I know my British history." It was true, he was often better at recalling British facts than Iain was despite being a history teacher, "I know about a massacre that happened in 1910, in a small hermit village in amongst the Grampian Mountains. One man visited the village and slaughtered every last man, woman, and child before setting the entire village on fire, killing all the livestock and destroying every last bit of the village, effectively ending the existence of Kirkfale, it was never rebuilt for superstitious fears. So, I ask you again, Iain, and I want the truth this time, where are you living in Scotland?" Iain sensed the disapproving tone of his father; he had used it many times in his childhood, and he suddenly realised he used that same tone in class.

"Honestly, Dad, we are living in Kirkfale. I work at the boarding school and Mary owns a shoe shop in the high street." He had nothing else to say, he was telling the truth.

"Fine! If you don't want to tell me, that's your prerogative, but may I suggest you do not make up fabricated lies to show how much you hate me." The line went quiet and for a moment amongst his surprise, Iain thought his father had put the phone down, but he could hear his faint breathing.

"Look," Iain finally said, "I have no idea what just happened there, but I am telling you the truth, Mary and I moved to Kirkfale several months ago when the mayor invited Mary to open up a shoe-making shop in the village. It was an offer too good to refuse; she jumped at the chance, particularly since she had just been refused a loan from the bank. I really don't know what you are implying, but what I'm saying is the truth." He hoped he was stating the truth firmly enough.

Finally, after a few more seconds of quietness his father spoke, "If that is the case and you and Mary are really living in Kirkfale, would you mind clarifying something for me?"

"Sure."

"Can you tell me why the hell you are living in a village that has been lying in ruins for the past century?" However, Iain had no chance to respond before his father severed the phone line, leaving him wondering what had just happened.

9

Staring blankly at the wall, Iain dropped the phone onto the side cabinet. It landed with a clatter and sat awkwardly in its charger, its red recharge light dithering on and off, not quite sure which way to go. A thousand thoughts went through Iain's mind. He knew, of course, there was only one way to prove his father was wrong – research.

He turned and retreated back to the comfortable chair his wife had left him in some time ago and pulled out his laptop from its carry-bag next to the chair, switched it on and waited for it to boot up. The only explanation Iain could think of to justify his father's comment was that he had meant another place. That being said, Iain could not get out of his head his father's voice saying Grampian Mountains.

Although his British geographical knowledge was quite limited, Iain guessed it would be too much of a coincidence to have two villages of the same name in so close a proximity.

He typed in the search parameters and pressed enter, within seconds there was a list of links to various websites and a quick check at the top of the page confirmed well over 13 million hits in total. He was half in his mind to call his father back and tell him to search for Kirkfale and see for himself, but something caught his eye. Under the sponsored sites list he read:

*Centenary Celebrations, Kirkfale
Tour the site of the largest
Massacre in Scottish history.*

He clicked the link and another window opened revealing a company from Aberdeen who specialised in Scottish tours with a difference. He scanned the page and identified many of the tours to be based on ancient burial sites around Scotland, all the major cities were included for their ghost walks, and several of the Scottish castles and stately homes were listed as alternative party venues. It did not take him long to find what he was looking for, KIRKFALE, 1910.

He clicked the link and was taken to another page detailing the massacre of Kirkfale in 1910. "As the story goes," he read, "it is believed that a stranger from the South visited the largely unknown village of Kirkfale in 1908 and during the two years following got to know every last villager, all except one who fled from the village in 1910. Not much is known from that point on, but rumours that are rife all-around Scotland, depict the stranger wielding a sword and slaughtering the entire village populace, men, women and children. It is not known what happened to this stranger or why the village suddenly erupted in fire and burned to the ground, but many scholars and researchers alike pertain this story to the old Scottish folklore of Black Donald."

The cursor hovered over 'Black Donald' and it changed to a link. His intrigue urged him to click the mouse button. He did and was taken to another page, this time the title read:

Scottish Legends and Folklore

He continued reading, "Black Donald is an ancient folklore believed to originate in the early part of the 12th century. The story tells of a figure dressed in black who went around Scotland learning the trades of every man in order to become master of them all. The story describes Black Donald as having the ability to take on many different forms to get into the hearts of the Scottish people and learn their skills before taking them as part of his own.

"There is one version where this black figure failed to learn the skill of basting, making it hard for him to walk the vast Scottish Countryside. Another version depicts Black Donald as an ancient warrior who was tortured by the English King and forced to kill Scottish men, women and children against his will. However, it is widely believed that Black Donald's ghost haunts villagers across the length and breadth of Scotland causing unexplained deaths. Indeed, over the centuries, there have been many sightings of a figure dressed in a black robe that trails to the ground. The most famous sighting was Ki…"

The phone rang, interrupting his deep concentration. His immediate guess was that his father had recalled apologising. No doubt he, too, had researched Kirkfale and found that it was still standing with not a scorch mark in sight. He stood and walked over to the phone and read the caller ID; it was a Kirkfale code, but he did not recognise the number. Clearly not his father, unless, he mused, he had suddenly travelled all that way up in a rocket ship. He fought the urge to smile as he pressed the green button and held the phone to his ear, "Hello?"

"Iain, you better get down here," said a frantic female voice.

"Who is this?" Visions of practical jokes flooded his mind.

"Maggie MacGilley, your wife's shop is on fire." He could sense the urgency in her voice and concluded she was telling the truth.

"Is Mary, ok?"

"I don't know, Son. Oh man it's awful, you gotta get down here." The phone went dead.

"Maggie? Hello, Maggie?" He threw the phone down and shot for the door, grabbing his coat on the way. A pain shot up through his leg, but he ignored it, he had to; Mary was in trouble.

*

The smouldering carcass that was once MARY'S SHOES still gave off a surprising amount of heat. Iain could not help but sweat even from his sitting position on the other side of the road. As the smoke stung his nostrils and tears welled up in his eyes, Mrs Deary approached and sat down beside him offering a tissue. He reluctantly took it and immediately felt embarrassed, "The smoke got into my eyes."

"Sure, Dear, I understand." She patted him on the shoulder as he blew his nose making a sound like a trumpet.

His wife, the woman he loved, was likely lying dead in a burnt outbuilding and there was absolutely nothing he could do except wait and that infuriated him. Every so often, despite his despair, he wiped his face with his soggy sleeve to get the stinging sweat and tear mix out of his eyes.

The fire had already been extinguished and the walls revealed evidence of a burning with scorch marks surrounding the windows and doorway. The shell of the building reminded him of an old picture from a history book about the blitz that he had taught so many times. He never for once believed he would ever see such a building first hand. He fought another sniff back, ignoring the whispers behind him.

Taking his eyes off the smoking wreck for a moment, he surveyed the villagers standing on the street watching the fire brigade finish their duties. Many of them had restrained him when he arrived, to stop him entering the burning building. He wondered if anyone had either started the fire or had seen the culprit start it.

One thing he was sure about, this was no accident. He returned his gaze back to the commotion and sat up as several firemen left the building and stood in front of their senior officer to report what they had found. Although Iain could not hear what they were saying, he could tell it was not good news from the shaking of heads and the periodic looks toward him. "She can't be dead; she just can't be!" He jumped up and started towards the firefighters but was held back by one or two people, "Why won't they tell me anything?"

He looked back at the villagers, some of the older women held their hands to their mouths aghast, as their husbands held their shoulders. It was clear this village was a close-knit community, who all cared for each other, but there was something not right. Something that did not sit all too well with Iain, but before he could figure it out, he was interrupted, "Here Son, I've made you a cup o' tea, extra sweet. It's good for the shock, you ken." Iain turned to see Mrs Doherty holding a tray with a teapot, one cup and a plate of chocolate biscuits. He did not fancy eating at the moment, but the tea did sound a good idea. He nodded, took the tray, placed it next to him on the path and poured himself a drink, before turning back to the rubble with a cup in his hand. The thoughts of something strange, a distant memory.

Just like in the many movies that Iain had taken Mary to watch when they had been courting, the next few seconds as a fireman approached from the wreckage, seemed to Iain, to take place in slow motion. He was looking directly at Iain. He knew what that meant. His fingers became rigid, and the cup slid from his hand and smashed on the road between his feet, hot tea splashing all over his shoes, but that was the last thing on his mind. Scrambling to his feet and wanted to meet the fireman halfway, but he could not move from his spot. "Mr. Cameron," the officer began removing his helmet, "the fire fighters have discovered the remains of someone and by the dimensions it looks like a woman, now," he quickly said to prevent Iain jumping to any premature conclusion, "that does not automatically mean that they are the remains of your wife, but the likelihood is…" Iain just stared at the officer as if his world had just been flushed down a toilet, "Sir, I AM terribly sorry."

"Do you know what started the fire?" Iain mouthed without any conviction. His eyes fell on the smoking building and the body that was being bagged up by the firemen.

"It's too early to say at the moment, but we can definitely say it started in the back, near the back entrance. We will need a forensics team to come in and confirm the location and the cause; you will receive a full report when one is completed." The fire officer looked back at the shell of the building and then back to Iain, "I suggest you go home and rest, call family, friends, anybody who can come and support you at this time." He patted Iain on the shoulder, "I am terribly sorry for your loss," and returned to the building and his work.

*

From the far side of the street, just behind the parked ambulances and fire engines, a lone figure dressed in a uniform looked on as the proceedings unfolded. He should have got involved given his perceived position but chose to stay clear for the time being. It was not yet time for him to start, but that time, he knew, was not far off. He checked his old-fashioned watch that hung from a chain attached to the inside pocket of his tunic, and nodded, "Now it begins."

10

"Do you Iain James Cameron take Mary Lucy Welsh to be your lawfully wedded wife, to have and to hold, in sickness and in health from this day forward, forsaking all others?" asked the vicar standing just in front of Iain and Mary.

Iain remembered being nervous as he watched his wedding DVD. He also remembered an argument with Mary about making the DVD; HE thought it was a waste of time and money. He was glad she had won the argument, otherwise he would have nothing to remember her by, other than his memories, but he surmised even they fade over time. A tear formed in his eyes making the film blurry and causing him to instinctively sniff.

"I do."

"And you, Mary Lucy Welsh, do you take Iain James Cameron to be your lawfully wedded husband to have and to hold, in sickness and in health from this day forward, forsaking all others?" the vicar said to Mary.

Through his tears, he could just make out the nervous look Mary gave Iain before answering and heard the soft grind in the back of her throat as she tried to clear it.

"I do."

Iain threw the scrunched-up tissue onto the floor to join the numerous other pieces of tissue that had been haphazardly thrown, soggy from nose-blowing and crying. A box of half-empty tissues lay on the coffee table next to the opened wedding album. A picture of Mary in her unforgettable wedding dress looked back up at Iain bearing her sweet smile. He remembered how he wanted to make sure everything was just like she had imagined it as a child. He was glad when her face brightened up like a child opening a present on Christmas Morning and finding the one thing he or she had asked for.

"You may kiss the bride," the vicar said smiling.

Iain watched as the two figures reached in and embraced for the first time on that day and kissed a long, passionate kiss. He closed his eyes and tried to savour that moment. Struggling, he held on to something that gave him warmth. Her lips were sweet and warm, soft and caring and sent a million tingles through his nerves. It was like no other kiss he had ever experienced and would be like no other he would experience again.

"Mary!" He cried, "Why did you go back to the shop? Why did *I* let you go?"

The phone rang.

He ignored it, now was not a time to talk to anyone, he just wanted Mary back. It stopped after a few rings, but Iain did not care. He watched as the newly married Mr and Mrs Cameron walked down the aisle with cheers, claps, and massive smiles on their faces. The tune to *'All you need is love'* bellowed from a musical combo organised by his best man. They had no cares for the future; everything would work out for them, because they had love. Right on cue, the DVD sounds faded and was replaced by the Beatles Classic, 'ALL YOU NEED IS LOVE', Mary's favourite song. He smiled as he remembered the discussion between Mary and him about the song going on the wedding DVD. He had eventually given in to her after she had put on a major sulk and stopped talking to him.

"I'm so sorry, Sweetheart I could not be there for you; I've let you down so much."

The phone rang again, Iain ignored it again. He really did not want to talk to anyone, but for some reason this time, whoever it was, was being persistent. The phone continued to ring and despite Iain trying hard to blot it out of his mind, he could not, and the noise punched through into his thoughts making him stir.

He stomped over and picked up the receiver, but it stopped just as he pressed the connect button. Tutting, he looked at the caller ID, but his focus was drawn away when a knock sounded from the front door. The setting was typical of an old horror movie he had watched as a child, the scene just before the villain bursts in and attacks the girl. That, however, was fiction, he reminded himself as the knock on the door echoed around the house again.

Walking to the door still holding the phone, he slowly opened it half expecting a boogie man to pounce on him but was confronted instead by a dark figure dressed entirely in black with a cloak that reached the ground. His gloved hands were holding an elaborate walking stick in front of him, but not, Iain noticed, for support, but rather for show. The visitor's hood covered his face perhaps to protect the owner from the fierce rain. He spotted how the drops bounced vivaciously off his hood and shoulders like the tiny drops were hitting a trampoline. #

He stepped forward to block the doorway and immediately felt numerous pinpricks stab his cheek with such force that pain surged in his face. Despite the rain pelting down, the figure did not move urging Iain to ask, "Yes?" He really could not think of anything else to say, although now that he had said that thousands of things flashed in his mind.

"Iain how are you doin'?" the mysterious figure asked with his familiar Scottish twang. He instantly recognised the voice from the corridors of the school, "Are you no' goin' to invite me in? It's a terrible night." His low, monotonous voice rumbled through the air like a clap of thunder.

"Of course, please come in, what brings you out here at this hour and," Iain looked up as if to see the source of the rain, "in this weather?" He sniffed and allowed the figure to walk in. Iain did not offer to take his cloak or stick, as he had already decided the headmaster was not going to stay too long. He wanted to be alone. He was glad, however, when the figure lowered his hood and confirmed his identity.

"I trust you are coping." The headmaster said looking round, "When I was informed of your wife's death, I came as quickly as I could to pass on my condolences."

"It is not necessary, Mr Black," Iain said with an absent mind, despite not being in the workplace, Iain felt compelled to still call him Mr as opposed to his first name. The man has an air about him that somehow commanded instant respect from everyone.

"No, but I did, all the same, you are, after all, one of my valued staff. It is in my best interest to ensure all staff receive the appropriate care and support, particularly if they experience challenging times that could influence their performance."

"Look, I appreciate the gesture, I truly do, but I would rather be alone at the moment." Iain moved his hand towards the door handle but stopped when the headmaster spoke again.

"I also came to see if you would come back to work."

Iain froze and continued looking at the door handle, a million things ran through his mind, not least of which was for him to swing around and plant a fist on the elderly man's cheek for suggesting such a thing. He straightened up and looked back at the elderly man, "Sorry? Did you not hear my wife died today?"

"Aye, I did, in fact, I know from experience if you stay here in your home focusing on nothing but that you become far worse than if you returned to work, immediately." That was enough to push Iain over the edge, and he felt a mini explosion in his mind.

He opened the door, still looking at the headmaster. "I think it's time you left. I WON'T be coming back to that school now or ever, consider this my resignation, effective immediately!" Iain's anger roared from every orifice in his head, but he could only muster growling through his teeth.

Black continued staring at Iain for what seemed a long moment, if he was at all affected by the sudden outburst, he did not show signs of any. Instead, he nodded. That made Iain even angrier, he wanted to rip his throat out, but something stopped him, something held him to the spot. His body was so rigid it felt paralysed where he could only control his eyes. All he could do, despite the ferocious rage that filled every molecule of his being, was watch the headmaster raise his hood and walk towards the door.

"Aye, I'm not here to demand anything of you and am not insensitive to your current situation." Iain's eyes widened, "There is no need to work your notice, I wish you well in your future, Iain, my deepest condolences for your loss." His voice seemed lower than a moment ago, it sounded like a deep throttle, "if you change your mind, Iain, be rest assured the job will still be there." Iain slammed the door more than he intended but did not care.

*

The dampness filled her nostrils. It was the putrid odour that made her nauseous and encouraged her to open her eyes. She felt groggy at best and tried to fight the urge to close her eyes again. She looked around but could see nothing but black darkness. Having no idea where she was or how she got there, she tried to stand, but soon realised the bangles she wore around her wrists and ankles were much more than just jewellery. Pain began stinging her wrists forcing her to writhe in agony and screw her eyes closed.

She slowly opened her eyes again and just looked ahead for a few moments to allow her eyes to acclimatise to the darkness. Before long the little pricks of light penetrated the darkness outlining part of a stone wall, puddles she hoped were not produced by humans and…

…nothing.

There was a smell of death about her, and she could just hear the distant drip of some liquid she presumed was water, just as a shiver rushed down her back.

Now, fear was setting in.

11

Anger continued to swell up inside Iain like a balloon being slowly filled with air. He was on the verge of yelling but knew that would solve absolutely nothing, particularly since there was no one to hear him scream. Instead, he just sat, glass of whiskey in hand looking out the window. The wedding DVD had long since been stopped, the album closed and his sadness for his wife's recent death was manifesting as hatred for every person in the entire village of Kirkfale, especially the headmaster.

    The dark clouds looked as heavy as Iain's head hovering over the entire village, most of which Iain could see from his panoramic floor-to-ceiling front window. The rain that fell from each cloud pounced on everything, smothering it, saving nothing. He could not remember such a bad night since moving to Scotland. He chastised himself for allowing the whole move to go forward. He should have seen it was too good to be true. He should have put his foot down, but that would have denied her this once in a lifetime chance to make her happy.

His laptop blipped. He ignored it, so caught up in his emotional roller-coaster that he had no interest in its message. A tear emerged from his left eye and found its way over the contours of his cheek reaching his chin before forming a drip that fell into his glass of whiskey. He had to leave. There was nothing holding him to the God-forsaken village of Kirkfale.

Standing from his chair, he walked to the cabinet. He grabbed the half-filled whiskey bottle and returned to the chair. He poured a healthy portion and set the bottle on the coffee table next to the opened laptop. Taking the glass, he swirled the whiskey around. He hated whiskey without ice, but since there was no method of making ice quickly, the drink would have to do without the 'rocks'. Glancing at the laptop, he skimmed the email headings. A new email with the subject, 'Kirkfale 1910', jumped out at him. He deleted it immediately without opening it. He had had enough; he had already decided to leave Kirkfale behind. His wife was dead. He was now alone. There was nothing left tying him here. His father's comment earlier popped into his head, and he began wishing the story was real.

The laptop blipped again. He downed the whiskey.

*

He opened his eyes unaware he had drifted off. Licking his lips, he realised he was thirsty, TOO MUCH WHISKEY, his head began to pound like a drum, NOT ENOUGH WHISKEY. Rubbing his eyes to clear the sleep, he yawned, stretching his arms and legs as far as he could. He grabbed the glass and downed the remainder of whiskey. Placing the glass back on the table, Iain's eye caught sight of four unopened emails with the last one in capital letters:

KIRKFALE MASSACRE – READ!!!

He deleted them immediately. He was passed caring. As soon as the messages disappeared however, another appeared, saying the same as the last one. He was about to click the delete link when his mobile began to signal a message received. He did not believe in coincidences, but that spooked him a little.

Grabbing his phone, he sighed at the absence of an ID number and then read, "OPEN EMAIL, LOOK AT IMAGE, YOUR FRIEND." He blinked and shook his head in disbelief. Some people were evil to play on the emotions of those who were grieving. Looking at the text, he struggled to make sense of it. His eyes flicked over to his laptop. The bold heading seemed to flash at him, urging him to click on it. After a few more moments, he moved the cursor over the email heading and clicked the bin icon.

He poured another glass of whiskey and downed it in one. He blinked and coughed before wiping his mouth and placing the empty glass back on the table. His throat felt warm, his breath momentarily taken from him, but it forced himself to focus. He read the text again just as his laptop blipped again with another email telling him to click now. Sighing, "Well, whoever you are, you are persistent. I'll give you that!" He clicked the email to open, figuring he had nothing else to lose.

An image appeared of a group of people circling an individual in the centre holding a sword. He identified the clothes from the early part of the 20th century and the long, slender sword, a traditional

Scottish Warrior sword he guessed, the name of which eluded him, but he could not think of any reason why anyone would send it to him. He checked again; the sender was anonymous. CONVENIENT! He had no idea what to make of the image and was about to close the laptop when he received another text. What the…? Something made him feel uneasy as he read his phone:

Img 1910, C any1 U knw?

He concentrated for a while, he had not got used to text language, as much as Mary had. He smirked at remembering the times when she texted him using text language, and he found it hard to decipher. At times, he had to ask a kid from his class to translate much to his embarrassment. "Image 1910, c…" he thought for a second, "Oh, see anyone you…" He tried thinking of something that would fit the last few letters but came up blank every time. Reaffirming his dislike for text language. Choosing to forget the last word, he turned back to the image.

"Image 1910, see anyone…" concentrating hard, he started with the central figure holding the sword. He could not think of how he would know anyone back in 1910, but everything up until now had been too bizarre not to continue.

He froze.

His breathing stopped momentarily, or at least he thought it did. He consciously felt his throat and lips become dry. The central figure gradually stood out from the rest, not because of the sword, not because the person was standing in the middle slaughtering everyone else, but something far more obvious. His eyes slowly followed the figure's cloak from his head to the ground and… "No! It can't be!" Shaking his head, he squashed his eyes with the heel of his hands. What his mind was telling him was preposterous, absolutely ridiculous.

He rubbed his eyes with clenched fists, this time. The image seemed to have burned itself on the back of his eyelids and he could see it even with his eyes firmly closed. He opened them again and pushed the laptop back and stood. Before long the urge to pace was too great, and he took several steps towards the kitchen door and back again, running through everything he had witnessed and discovered with every step.

After pacing several times, he knelt down to the table, turned the laptop and opened the internet and clicked on a bookmark he saved earlier on. When the page came up, he scrolled down to what he was looking for and read, "Indeed, over the centuries, there have been many sightings of a figure dressed in a black robe that trails to the ground. The most famous sighting was in 1910 in the village of Kirkfale, in the valleys of the Grampian Mountains. It is said that this mysterious, black-robed figure slaughtered the entire village except for one and then burned the village to the ground." His mind was on over-drive, too many thoughts to process, but he had to quickly put the pieces together. I ignored his logical mind, screaming that the whole idea was stupid.

He looked back at the image and just concentrated on the man in the middle and for the first time he realised his facial features. His hair was grey and short, and his face wrinkly. His nose was nothing special, but was dwarfed, not in size but in presence, by his dark, black eyes. Even though the picture was older that Iain, he could not help but think the eyes were looking straight at him.

His phone beeped signifying another text message.

*"Check out woman on left,
Any1 U know? She's alive!*

"Woman on left?" He shrugged and returned to the picture and searched for a woman on the left and spotted several, or at least from his copy, it looked like several, a few, he decided, could be wearing kilts. After scrutinising all the people on the left and almost resigning himself to how ridiculous the whole thing had become, a face of a young woman popped out from between two heads. He could have sworn she had not been there moments before, but he knew that was impossible, since the picture was painted several decades ago.

The face of the woman was much smaller than the others since it was being largely covered by the bodies of the other people. Iain magnified the section of the painting and waited for it to refocus. Seconds later, he jumped back and continued frantically crawling backwards until his head hit an object. His eyes did not move from the magnified section of the picture and neither did he blink. He felt his heart thump in his chest, but he ignored it. He froze for several minutes before slowly moving closer to laptop and picture, as if that would make the picture clearer, "No it can't be…" he whispered.

The phone signalled another message, but it did not register in his mind, instead he was staring, too intently, at the woman on the photo of the Kirkfale Massacre in 1910. Total confusion reigned. The mass of alcohol would not have helped, although now, he needed more to grasp what had just

transpired. With all his agony, frustration and disbelief, he only uttered one word…
"Mary!"

12

When the laptop finally went dark to save power, Iain felt the blood seep back into his ankles urging him to move. Mary was no longer looking at him from a picture taken in 1910 and he was now able to move his legs. He shuffled slowly back to the table and picked up his phone that had been beeping for ages and read the text.

It must be 2nite for Mary!

The text made little sense to Iain, so he pushed the phone into his jeans pocket, grabbed his coat, and headed out into the dismal night rain.

He had no plans, but he knew he just had to do something. If indeed the text from the stranger was true and Mary was alive, he had to get her back, somehow. He paused momentarily before starting the car, who could help him make sense of all the information in his head? Finally, he nodded and turned the key. The engine ignited effortlessly allowing him to set off immediately. He had made a decision, one he would most probably regret later, but one he had no choice in making; he just hoped, his fears were not going to come true.

Despite the bleak darkness, the road felt alive with the movements of the tree branches that swayed ferociously like a troupe of wild dancers, flailing in front of Iain as he drove, their shadows clawing at his windscreen. The car's headlights created ghostly images that seemed to join in with the dance as the rain played the percussion on his car roof. He hated driving at night in the rain, at least in the snow, you could see the hazard. He consciously held the steering wheel at ten o'clock and two o'clock, maintaining control, his knuckles turned white, and pain shot up his arms. The last thing he or Mary needed was for HIM to crash. If he crashed, all this would be for nothing and even in the slimmest of hopes he had about saving Mary would be gone.

The car swerved, forcing Iain to compensate. He imagined he was fighting against some hidden force, bent on stopping him doing what he was about to do. He slammed on the brakes when a fallen tree jumped out of the darkness blocking the road. Watching for a moment as the rain drops, visible by way of his lights, bounced off the car's bonnet in every direction. He had narrowly missed a thick branch that was pointing into the road like a long, sharp finger. He took a deep breath and drove around the obstacle and continued down the road towards the village centre, picking up speed as he drove. He could not afford to be delayed any longer.

He had only travelled a few hundred yards when the rain became so severe that it blocked his vision. He took his foot off the accelerator and allowed the car to slow gently. He refused to stop; however, Mary needed him, and he had to hope it was not too late. Rounding the corner and snatched a view of the darkened school in the distance; it was large, even from that point, was it his imagination, or did it look more sinister at night? He shook his head and returned his focus to the road and stepped on the brakes again, swerving to the right and narrowly missing something in the road.

"What the ...!" He shouted trying to regain control of the car as it entered into a daring spin. Within a terrifying moment, the engine stalled, bringing him to a stop. Chest heaving, he turned back to look but saw nothing. He hadn't felt a bump or knock. He grabbed the torch from the glove box and got out of the car.

He opened the door, and the rain began inflicting its painful blows. Tiny pinpricks pelted his legs even through his thick jeans. He grimaced and turned up his coat collar.

Hunching his shoulders, he tried to ignore the pain; he had to for Mary's sake. Iain swooped the torch over the road but could only see, barely, the hedge that lined the road and the trees behind them. He took several steps forward, pushing hard against the wind. He could have sworn he saw something large in the road, but there was nothing there. Shaking his head, he wiped the rain from his face and turned round jumping as he did. The torch clanged on the ground ad Iain took a step back to steady himself.

Looking into a furry-rimmed hood, Iain was surprised to see the face of an elderly woman peering back at him. He steadied himself in time to hear her voice, "I'm not goin to stop you going up there, but a word of warning, Son, you watch your back. That devil is an affy cunning creature and wants you for his own. Remember this though, you are *not* alone, you have never been alone, and you never will be alone. We'll help you get up there, but once inside, you, and only you, can slay the beast." She turned and faded into the darkness, aided by her black raincoat.

"Wait...who are you? What beast? Come back!" But she had gone. His coat flapped violently in the wind and the rain smacked the back of his head, he could hear the car's engine and see the headlights as bright as they were before he skidded around the lady. Then is dawned on him "Didn't I stall?"

*

Driving through the village gave Iain the creeps. Every building was dark, the streetlamps were not working, and the trees were swaying in every direction at the command of the wind. The rain fell in defiance to anything that got in its way and soaked without compromise or prejudice. Iain's wipers were on full, and he was still struggling to see through the river gushing from his roof. He could not remember the last time he drove in such stormy weather, but needs were a must and Mary was definitely worth it.

Eventually he came through the other side of the village and turned the corner towards the school, largely obscured from view due to the swaying trees. Having driven that particular road many times already, he estimated it would only be a few minutes before it became visible and then only a few more minutes before he reached the long drive leading to the school, itself.

Up ahead were two points of light blocking his road, he could only assume they belonged to a car, since everything behind them was invisible through the heavy rain. He slowed ready to stop, just in case someone needed his help to move a stranded car, although not an ideal situation to find himself in. Suddenly, red and blue lights began flashing silently to signal for Iain to pull over. Worried the police officer would smell the alcohol on his breath, he reluctantly pulled safely to the side. A lone figure in a large rain coat and hat, approached on foot. A splash with each step.

Iain pressed the button to lower the window as he watched the officer walk round from the front of the car. The white lights of the police car silhouetted the officer. A face suddenly appeared from the darkness close to the window, Iain recognised him.

Trying to keep his head back to avoid the sting of the rain and revealing his alcohol-smelling breath, Iain said, "What's the problem, Officer?"

The officer leant forward and rested his hand on the roof of the car, Iain was thankful he was providing some respite from the rain, "The road ahead is flooded, and it's impassable."

"But I need to get through…" He remained calm, even though he was frustrated, he did not want to give the officer an idea he had been drinking. He consciously forced his head to maintain contact with the head rest of his seat.

"Well if you go that way," he pointed towards a road that went off to the side. It had rarely been used being a single-track lane with a sheer drop on one side and given it was dark and stormy, it would be 100 times worse, "you will bypass the obstruction and get to the school quicker."

"The school?"

The policeman smiled, tapped the rim of his hat and said, "You be sure to be careful now, Mr Cameron, your next few hours are going to be trying for you, be strong." Before he could reply or make sense of what he had just heard, the officer had turned and disappeared into the rain. Iain raised the window.

Continuing to look at the lights for a moment longer, the wipers furiously dashed from side to side, suddenly breaking into his focus. On another occasion they would annoy him, and he rarely put them on that fast for that reason, but today was different. He blinked back to reality and set off down the alternative route.

Within a matter of minutes, faster than Iain anticipated, he arrived at the back entrance of the school, hidden behind heavy foliage and bushes. He turned the lights off so as to escape detection from anything that could be patrolling the grounds. He did not think why that would be the case, but since everything had already happened the way it had, it was better to be safe than sorry. Just as he turned the lights off, his phone broke the quietness and made Iain jump slightly. He took his phone out his pocket and read the message,

To save Mary, reveal
BD by feet

"BD? Who the hell is BD?" The complexities of the recent set of messages were confusing him. He had had enough. He threw the phone to the passenger seat, but it hit the floor instead. He didn't care; he had somewhere he had to be. Opening the car door, he stepped out. The rain still pouring, though it seemed softer, somehow. He switched the torch on and ran to the school entrance.

13

The big iron door reminded Iain of an old castle drawbridge and at first glance appeared immovable, but he knew different. He grabbed the cold, wet handle and turned pushing with his other hand. Initially, the door moved slowly and creaked in complaint. Eventually, it moved much more easily and was surprisingly light for its size. Stepping inside, he lowered the collar of his coat and looked back out into the night rain. At least the officer was right, I wasn't detected; at least I don't think I was. He turned back to the foyer of the school, large, grand and illuminated by candles. He assumed the electricity was off and the school caretakers had gone round lighting the candles, but frankly, he really did not care.

    He looked round and remembered the last time he stepped foot in the school; the day he returned home after witnessing that ritual. It had appeared far different than it presented itself just now. The shadows jumped and danced as the flames moved on each torch. It really was a nice and historic setting, but admiration would have to wait, he had a job to do.

Approaching the stairs, Iain was unaware the door had begun to swing shut. When his foot hit the bottom step, the slam echoed throughout the large stone foyer startling Iain and no doubt notifying any occupants of his arrival. He grabbed the banister to steady himself before looking back. Not knowing what to expect or why the door had slammed closed, he proceeded up the stairs.

He gripped the banister firmly, his knuckles turning white, when the pad of footprints sounded behind him. He was right to be concerned. As he turned to face the foyer, he was confronted with five robed figures that had appeared from the shadows. "You have got to be kidding me!" He yelled as the first of the five approached.

Each figure held a wooden staff and, other than the one now moving towards him, stood perfectly still. He could not see anyone's face for they were covered by their respective hoods. The one walking stopped about a metre away from Iain. Iain gulped. A moment later, the robed figure changed his stance and spun the staff several times, its final resting place being that of a position ready to strike. Fully intimidated, Iain spun around and scaled the stairs three at a time, hoping the hooded figures would not follow.

As he approached the top of the stairs he looked up and stumbled. Waiting for him were five hooded figures. He quickly considered his options, there were none. He could not go back in case they were still waiting for him downstairs, and he could not proceed because of these five. He regained his balance and watched as the central figure approached him, again. He stopped and took up an attacking posture as before. This time, however, Iain had nowhere to run; he was going to have to fight.

Conscious that his only experience of combat was fencing, he resigned himself to believing his days were numbered. The lone figure advanced and swung his staff. Iain dodged once, twice and felt the brunt of the third blow in his abdomen. Immediately, he felt the wind escape him, but had little time to think about it. The staff swung again, hitting him square in the nose. The force of the blow sent him flying backwards, and he hit the stone floor with a resounding thud.

He grabbed his nose and felt the warm sensation of blood trickle down his nostril. Wiping it away with his sleeve, he looked up at his assailant and although his blood was boiling with anger, he could not see any way to defeat him. His entire body was crying out in protest as he got to his feet. He looked around for something he could use as a weapon. Within seconds, the figure advanced and struck a blow with such force, Iain was thrust backwards into the bookcase that lined the corridor wall. The shelves broke under his weight and old dusty books piled on top of him, He stole a look at the other four figures behind the fighter, still standing motionless.

Iain stood up once more, not sure where his strength was coming from or when it would fail. Despite the obvious areas of pain, he figured he should be in far more pain than he was and was thankful. The attacker swung his staff again making contact with Iain's head and forcing him to stumble. He was aware the staff narrowly missed his eye; he could only imagine what damage a blow like that could have done to his sight; but defiantly, he stood again. However, diving between a small gap in the bookcases, he made the most of a flash of opportunity to gather a deep breath and regain his composure. The staff swept toward him again, but narrowly missed him, striking the top shelf causing the books to scatter like toppled dominoes.

"Who are you? What do you want with me?" There was no response, except the fighter turned to face the others. Iain guessed they were talking through some form of telepathy but reasoned that was impossible. Regardless, the four companions joined their leader and took up similar stances before him. Whatever was keeping him from being badly hurt, he knew it would not last forever. He was rapidly running out of time.

Iain looked at the five fighters that now were poised to attack, "Well this is fair folks, five against one!" He did not smile, but his eyes kept darting from one assailant to the other. It seemed an eternity before there was any further movement from anyone other than Iain.

As they advanced simultaneously, Iain had only one thought, DUCK!

14

A brilliant white light appeared, so bright that it engulfed everything and illuminated every shadow hiding behind every object. Iain closed his eyes and covered them with his arms, hoping he would still be alive at the end of it. There was no heat, no sound, nothing except the light which disappeared just as quickly as it had appeared and returned the first-floor landing back to the darkness it was moments before. Iain slowly opened his eyes and cautiously moved his hands away from his face and gasped. He surveyed the five motionless bodies that lay before him. "What the…?" Shaking his head, he approached the nearest one, it could have been the one who attacked initially, but he was not sure, they all looked the same in their black robes.

He knelt down and lifted the hood over the head of the body and instantly recognised the attacker as the farmer from the top of the village, Gallagher. Iain was shocked to say the least. The last time he had seen Gallagher was at Mary's shop opening, he was offering children lifts in his tractor. He moved to the next figure and reached out to lift the hood, but stopped when he got an overwhelming urge to move.

Whether it was fear, a drive to save Mary, or some other thing, Iain moved toward the next flight of stairs.

He reached the top of the steps and stopped briefly to catch his breath, although he knew he could not stay too long. His chest was heaving and sweat drenched his forehead, but he had to go on. He removed his long coat and threw it to the floor without a second glance and continued. Feeling and over-riding sense of determination, he mustered up enough energy to start jogging.

Halfway down the corridor, Iain heard a soft sniff, stopping he looked around and spotted a small boy crying. Despite the circumstances, he WAS a teacher, albeit one without a job, his sense of duty outweighed any other feelings he might have. Still breathing heavily, he approached the small boy, clearly a first-year student, although to Iain, it was slightly odd how he was still wearing a school uniform at THAT time of night, let alone being OUT at that time of night.

"Hey Buddy…" he took a deep breath, "What's up, why are you crying?" The little boy looked up. His face was wet with tears, suggesting he had been crying for some time. Iain put his arm on his shoulder, "Now whatever it is, we can sort it." Iain tried to smile despite what was on his mind. However, as Iain crouched down, the boy's eyes turned bloodshot, black rings appeared round his eyes and he began to snarl.

The boy leapt unnaturally from his position and landed on Iain. He snarled and punched Iain, repeatedly in the chest and face. Despite his size, the little boy threw quite a wallop, causing Iain's face to be severely bruised. Grabbing the arms of the boy, he pushed him off, before rolling to his side and standing up. His back was turned for only a second, but it was enough for the boy to pounce again. This time kicking and thumping his back and head. Still growling like a rabid dog.

Iain had had enough of this. This 'child' was clearly not human. He grabbed hold of the boy's legs, to secure him to Iain's shoulders and ran backwards, hitting the opposite wall, as planned. It only took one attempt before the boy went limp. Iain's heart exploded in agony when he set the boy down. If he ever got out of this alive, his future as a teacher would be over.

He waited a moment longer staring at the boy's lifeless body on the floor until something grabbed his peripheral vision. Turning, he looked down the corridor just long enough to see one candle go out. He raised an eyebrow, another torch went out, and another, and another. A noise that reminded Iain of a stampede echoed down the corridor, intensifying as the extinguished lights drew closer. He felt his heart throb in his head, he wanted to run but was frozen to the floor.

A herd of boys of all sizes was growing larger with every passing second. Iain shook his head, "What is going on in here?" He turned and ran the opposite way, thankful his legs started moving. He knew he did not have far to go and would be able to dodge the oncoming mob by stepping into the Head's office.

As he reached the door, he took hold of the handle and looked back at the approaching rabble and darkness. He pushed the door and fell through before slamming it behind him. He was not sure what he alone could do against the entire group of boys on the other side of the door but WAS grateful there was a door between him and them. It was a sturdy door, one that could take a lot of beating before giving way. He took some comfort in that.

Looking for the headmaster, he was disappointed when he could not see him. His office was lavish compared to the rest of the school's furniture. Chairs laced with gold thread, ornaments and vases of solid gold, or at least what looked like solid gold, and various other artefacts made of precious materials from platinum to diamond. There was a bookcase that extended the entire length of the wall with a spiral staircase heading upwards in the centre of the room. Next to that was a brass bust of a previous headmaster.

When he reached the spiral staircase, something prevented him from continuing. Something inside him was clutching at his senses and telling him not to go. Instead, he turned and took another careful look at the room. It was enormous, about the size of a tennis court. He had to smile when a thought of Mary owning a bedroom this size pooped into his head, she would find new and inventive ways to fill *every* available space.

He rested against the bust statue, and it moved. "Sheesh! How many secret passages does this castle have?" He watched as a portion of the bookcase moved backwards and off to the left, revealing a well-lit stairwell heading down. Without much thought, Iain knew instantly what he had to do.

15

Despite the fire torches burning at strategic positions down the spiral staircase, Iain could not help but feel a chill shoot down his spine. He shivered and his mother's voice flashed in his mind, '*someone walked over your grave, son*', only to brush the thought aside as nonsense. As he approached the bottom of the staircase, Iain felt his heart begin to beat faster and harder, so much so he could feel the thump in his wrists and hear the pounding in his ears. Sweat was forming little beads on his forehead and growing to form larger droplets that subsequently slid down his nose and dropped off the tip. He could not believe the humidity as he wiped his brow for the umpteenth time.

    He could hear faint voices down one of the corridors as he peered round the corner at the bottom of the steps. Gingerly he walked down the passageway, ensuring he made as little sound as possible. A million thoughts rushed through his mind. He stopped just shy of the wooden door leading to the room at the end of the corridor. It all seemed too familiar. The air was musty, but a familiar sweet flowery smell filled his nostrils. No matter how he tried, he could not place it. Eventually, he moved his head closer to the gap in the door.

A small chamber lay just beyond. It looked exactly like the one he had been in before, when he had his little 'accident' that had put him in hospital. Robed figures stood around a stone altar with their hands clasped in front of them and one stood before them on a platform addressing the others.

He moved his ear to the door to listen, "The time is almost upon us. We must ready ourselves for the transfer. You must clear your minds of all that will tarnish this glorious event." The voice was low, like a growl, but echoed throughout the chamber. Iain found the voice familiar somehow but, as with the smell, he could not place it. For a moment, however, he felt it came from behind him, though a quick check confirmed that not to be the case. "What is this? I can sense weakness among you." Iain could hear the elevated temper in his words, "I have waited one hundred years for this and will not let it slip through my fingers again. I will walk the Earth un-tethered. My Father will no longer have control over me!" Iain heard the animalistic fury in the last sentence, and, despite the aggression, he noticed the accent had lost its Scottish tones.

A figure eventually moved and looked up at the individual standing next to the stone altar, "My Lord," her voice sounded old, "I fear that my age is against me, I canna control my mind as I once could, please forgive me, my Lord."

The central figure nodded, "Then you should leave, your mind is weak and frankly, the stench is abhorrent." Iain watched the female nervously bow and turned to walk off, however, she did not get far before she was engulfed in flames. Mere seconds later, the flames and the body were gone, leaving the echo of her scream to linger just a moment longer.

A shiver went down Iain's back. "Are there any others who wish to join your cowardice sister on her journey to oblivion?" His voice stabbed through Iain like a sharp sword almost as if he were talking directly at him. He shook it off with another shiver that rippled across his shoulders and down his spine.

Then Iain's attention was drawn to the far side of the chamber, as another robed and hooded figure entered and bowed to the 'Lord'. "My Lord, I bring news of an intruder." His voice was younger, perhaps a teen from the school. The others turned their faces towards the new arrival. Iain scanned the faces he saw, but the headmaster was not amongst them. Some of the faces resembled villagers he met some time ago or so he thought.

"Have ye contained him?" The Scottish accent returned. Iain stiffened; had he been discovered? Things were becoming more and more bizarre. The man's accent the least of these.

The new arrival bowed his head, out of fear or reverence, Iain could not be sure. "I fear, my Lord, we have failed. The intruder is formidable, my Lord, he knocked The Five clean oot." The image of the five figures lying on the floor before him flashed in his mind. "His power is strong, my Lord, like only to yourself!"

There was a short silence before the lord spoke again, perhaps he was choosing his words carefully, or perhaps he was allowing his anger to rise up sufficiently, "FOOL!"

Iain watched as his gloved hand thrust forward toward the messenger. Immediately, he was lifted clean off the floor, his legs dangling like a rag doll. His arms clawed at his throat as if to pull a hidden cord from around his neck. The others did not move, though Iain thought he could see one or two taking small steps closer to the boy.As the boy dangled in mid-air, his hood slid clear of his head, Iain gasped. It was Bart, one of his tutees. Covering his mouth, eh hoped no one had heard him and was about to dodge back behind the door when he saw Bart's body fall limp. His arms fell like bricks to his sides followed shortly by his body crashing to the floor motionless.

"See what befalls anyone who fails me? Let this be a lesson to you all, I do not tolerate incompetence." His voice boomed throughout the entire chamber and beyond. "I am surrounded by weak-minded imbeciles!" He threw his hands up into the air. Instantly, several of the others erupted into flames and quickly vanished with screams of terror.

"My Lord, I shall go and find the intruder," said another male with an older voice as he stepped forward. He yielded a sword like none other Iain has seen before.

Iain spotted the Lord's black robe slowly ripple and twist as he turned his body towards the door Iain was crouched behind. He ducked back behind the door as quickly as humanly possible, but he could still hear, "That will not be necessary; it would seem our intruder has already found his way here." The words sounded lower and sharper than before. Another shiver shot down Iain's back as he put his head against a stone pillar.

"What have you got yourself into now, Iain?" he muttered under his breath.

Almost immediately, Iain felt a jab in his head urging him to raise his hands, "My Lord, I have found him," a young voice called from behind him. Iain began to move but received a smack on the back of his head, "Gonna no' do that you dunderheid! An' for killin' my father ..."

Another whack laid squarely on Iain's cheek sent him flying backwards into the rock and out cold.

16

"Bring in the shoemaker!" The words slipped faintly into Iain's ears as he lay on the cold floor. Whatever he had been hit with had been hard and knocked him out quickly for a few seconds. Now he felt like his thoughts were swimming against a thick tide of treacle.

A pain shot through his head from just above the right ear to his eye. He tried to lift his hand to explore his wound, but soon realised he was being held by two hooded assailants. Forcing himself to push the pain aside, he looked through the blood that dripped down over his eyelashes.

He was kneeling down at the front of the two holding him and facing the stone platform and altar. On the stage stood the one called, the Lord, still hiding his face with a hood and his hands with gloves. Others were standing facing the altar with their hands clasped in front of them.

"Brothers of the Order, we are about to embark on a new frontier, where we are free from our curse. On the stroke of midnight, it will be exactly one hundred years since we were last at this juncture, in this very village of Kirkfale. Glorious are ye who will witness the beginning o' a new era, my rebirth."

Iain could sense the enjoyment in the man's voice. He tried to think of whom the voice belonged to but was interrupted when there was scuffle to the left of him. Turning his head, he spotted three followers dragging a woman in a white lacy dress and wearing a cotton bag over her head. The dress reminded Iain of something worn at a wedding. He watched as the woman was roughly manhandled and laid upon the stone altar and strapped to the rock.

"Here, is our ticket to freedom, the key to the lock of our burden." The lord held out a hand towards the woman who was writhing and screaming. Iain willed her to break her bonds, but knew it was useless. He resigned himself to just watch as the lord walked to the woman's head. "Whilst I was here, one hundred years ago, you taught me your skill and talents and I paid you all handsomely, did I not?" There was a low-level murmur, "but one lass, by the name of Rose, escaped from the village back to her family in Argyll, cursing you all to spend eternity like this!"

An energy of excitement was growing in the followers, "She forced me to slaughter you all on that day." He grabbed the hood of the woman and yanked it off her head, "Behold, the descendant of Rose McFadgen, the shoemaker!" He held the head up for all to see.

Iain's heart sank a million miles, "MARY!" he shouted, struggling to free his hands, "Leave her alone or I *will* kill you all!" An empty threat, he knew, but with his emotions erupting into chaos he was not thinking straight.

The one calling the shots, slowly tilted his head just enough for Iain to glimpse his mouth and chin. The figure smiled, "Interesting demands from one not in a position to make demands." He let Mary's head hit the stone altar and took a few steps towards Iain, "You don't understand who I am, Iain, or what I am capable of doin."

"I know you are Black Donald or at least you believe you are. I know that Black Donald slaughtered every man, woman, and child of Kirkfale in 1910 and then burnt it down to the ground, just because Rose escaped. From that I suspect you are deranged and need psychological help." He spat at the feet of Black Donald. He tried to think of something else, figuring the longer he talked, the longer he had to think of a plan, and the longer Mary had to stay alive.

Donald laughed a deep, ear-piercing laugh before continuing, "When my freedom was postponed in 1910, I had to wait for a direct line of Rose McFadgen who had her look and skill to resume. Mary is that very descendant."

"But her name is not or never has been, McFadgen, her family are from Wales not Scotland," Iain pleaded.

"Mary was adopted as a baby when her Scottish family were killed by an act of God." Donald sniggered, though it sounded like a deep rattle, as if he was hiding something, "There are things going on here, your puny brain can't fathom. Forces beyond your comprehension. You will do well to leave it there and let me carry on."

"You can't possibly expect me..." Iain began angrily whilst struggling against his guards.

"I expect you will try your best, but you WILL fail. I brought Mary here to Kirkfale for the sole purpose of gaining her shoe-making skill, so that my skill set be complete, and I WILL be free."

"You talk as if you are the prisoner here." Iain's mind worked overtime to find something else to delay Donald's plans.

"Aye, that I am, but so are we all on this rock you call Earth."

Iain sniggered a little, but only enough to make his point, "Now you're talking as if you're an alien from out of space. Do you realise how pathetic you sound?"

"I am much more than you can imagine, Iain, so much more. Something I once offered you to partake in, and..." The Lord thought for a moment, "Yes, I will offer it to you again, just because I like your stamina." Donald stepped closer to Iain and with his left index finger under Iain's chin, pulled him up to a standing position. Iain knew those who were holding him gave him a 'gentle' nudge.

He now looked into the lord's hood and saw only the faint outline of a face. "Iain," he began quietly, "I am offering you immortality, where you can have whatever, your wildest dreams want. Anything you want will be yours for the taking and no one will stop you. I would give you the world to rule over if you wished it." Iain had noticed the Scottish accent had disappeared again, "All you need do is bow before me."

"And if I refuse?"

Donald chortled, "I'll kill you!" Iain continued staring at the darkness inside the hood but thought of Mary. He still had no options.

"Then I accept!" He smiled and watched as Donald nodded and turned back to the altar.

"Ye will come to realise the benefit of siding with me, Iain. In fact, in the next fifteen minutes we all will be set free of our curse and you all will receive your just rewards." Iain watched as Donald picked up a ceremonial dagger and said some incomprehensible incantation, before taking up position above Mary's body. As if an explosion of realisation occurred in his head, Iain's eyes widened.

"Who are ye really, Donald? I mean, are ye really Donald? How can ye have two accents, one Scottish when speakin' to your followers," Iain said in a rough dialect similar to Donald's, he hoped it would be sufficient, "and one when speaking to me?" he said in his normal accent. He hoped the difference was enough to punch through any brainwashing Donald had done to his followers.

He felt a nudge at his wrist and realised his wrist was free and without stopping to think, clenched it like a brick and swung. He made contact with the two holding him, knocking them down quite easily, but found others were charging upon him like a pack of wolves. A quick glance confirmed Mary was still alive, just before he was thrown to the ground by a larger follower. "Kill him!" A distant voice commanded.

Iain looked up as several more hooded fighters reached his side; it did not take long to work out the odds of success, but he thought of Mary, even as he received punches and kicks up and down his torso.

17

Once more, pain shot through his entire body. His nerves complained about working overtime as every punch and every kick made contact with some part of his flailing body. He knew his body would already be severely bruised, but before death ensued, he would suffer massive internal bleeding from many of his organs. He wanted to cry out in agony, but then realised the pain was subsiding.

His thoughts were interrupted by a feeling of weightlessness. He opened his eyes and almost jumped when he realised, he was floating in the air. However, within moments of his realisation, he was thrust against a far wall. Iain knew what had happened, but his mind was forced to think of something else when his helpless body smashed into the stone wall and crumpled to the floor. Despite what his body was going through, his one thought was giving him strength. The one thought that forces him to focus, which drove him to not give in.

Raising his head, Iain opened his eyes and looked at the followers; they were holding their positions. "Come on, finish it, you know you want to!" There must have been ten or twenty at first glance.

He scrambled to his knees, he barely had seconds before they could reach him and throw him against the wall again.

Iain heaved a sigh. He urged to cough. He could feel fresh blood-curdling at the back of his throat, a metallic stickiness. He resisted when he realised a sharp edge being slowly pressed against his neck. Looking down without moving his head, he saw the metal sword poised at his throat. He surveyed the blade; it was beautifully crafted with intricate designs weaving up and round the blade similar to wild ivy growing over a wall of a house. The design culminated at the base of the hilt which was hidden under the assailant's hand, but Iain could just make out a green emerald gem in a silver hoop at the tip of the hilt. "Nice." He could not help but admire the intricate design despite his predicament.

Without speaking a word, the assailant swung his sword. Iain grabbed the hilt pulled it clear of the assailant's hand. "Fool, you would have stood a better chance before giving me this." However, to Iain's surprise, the swordsman had already drawn another sword from his robe, almost identical in design to the one he now held, but instead of pointing it at Iain; he was pointing it at the others.

The swordsman raised his free hand and lowered his hood. Iain gasped when his only friend in Kirkfale revealed himself, "Andrew?" He dropped the sword with a clang.

Andrew turned his head, winked and smiled, "You're going to need that," he smiled before turning back to the mob. Grabbing the sword again, Iain took up a similar stance to Andrew.

"Who are you?"

"A friend..." that was all he could say before they both were lunged into battle.

Iain thrust the sword with expert precision; as if it were a foil, and he were fencing. Granted the sword was heavier, but the manoeuvres were just as effective, with the added bonus of piercing the flesh. Both he and Andrew danced as if they were following a practised recital as blade met flesh and splashed blood in every direction.

Pulling his sword out of the stomach of one assailant, Iain twirled and swiped at another's arm, cutting it clean off. This was followed closely by an elbow jab to the jaw, to throw the assailant off guard before stabbing him in the heart with the sword to finish the job. He dodged an incoming fist but allowed his sword to linger to his side just long enough to make contact with the attacker and slicing through his flesh until it reached bone. Iain slid the blade out of the falling man and headed for another.

It was not long before only Iain and Andrew stood panting with the swords readied for the next attack. They looked round and silently counted the bodies lying motionless at their feet. It had happened so fast, Iain could not believe it, the adrenalin had taken over, "Is it over?" he panted, hating the thought that he may have enjoyed that a little too much.

Andrew turned to him and smiled. His breathing was almost as quick as Iain's and just as heavy. He opened his mouth to say something but closed it again just as the sharp end of a sword erupted from his chest. Iain watched aghast as the blade continued to move forward and up, blood smearing on it and dripping off the tip. He could see in Andrew's eyes that he was not scared, but they soon glazed over, and his head slumped forward.

Iain watched the body of his friend as it hit the carpet of dead bodies. Pain and guilt filling his heart and mind, quickly replaced with a surge for revenge.

He looked up and saw the snarling grin of Black Donald. Hood down, eyes as red as blood and Iain froze. The headmaster! The mayor!

Anger burst his every vein, but he took up a defensive position with his sword ready to defend anyway, "You did not need to do that." His teeth were clenched giving a growl to his voice.

"This is my village *and* school; I have supreme power here. I can do whatever I want." Iain saw the corners of the headmaster's lips begin to curl up. Donald raised his sword, Andrew's blood still smeared on it. Everything was becoming clearer in Iain's mind.

"You knew about the sacrificial ritual down here, didn't you."

"It is necessary to bring them to my way of thinking, let's just say, it was an easy way to prepare the way for me."

"And the villagers? "It was all clear now. Iain chastised himself quietly for not seeing it before. He did not flinch from his defensive stance, however. He continued to stare at Donald, trying not to blink in case he missed him.

"Expendable resources." Donald curled the corners of his lips a little more and Iain felt nauseous, he fought it back down though. "These people lived and died at my command a hundred years before you were born. They are mind to do as I please."

"Who *are* you?" Although Iain was looking straight at Donald, his mind was still on Mary. "Whoever you are, I am going to take pleasure in going through you to save my wife." The smirk on Donald's face turned to a defiant grin.

"But what about *you*, Iain, *you* come here with hatred in your heart, killed all these people," he motioned to the bodies on the floor, "and still feel no regret. Something tells me you actually enjoyed it." He raised his free hand and pointed at Iain and laughed, "You did, didn't you, you actually found a thirst for killing people. That is *so* noble of you."

Iain took a step closer and pointed the sword at Donald, "I am not you!"

"Touch a raw nerve did I?" Donald stopped laughing and stepped forward. He looked at Iain for a moment longer before screwing his face into an angry growl and thrust his long, thin sword into Iain. It pierced his belly and lingered for a few seconds. Iain tried to knock the sword away with his own, but to no avail. All he achieved were several chimes of metal. Donald retracted the sword and thrust it into Iain's chest and twisted it and sneered.

Iain's lifeless body made no sound as it landed on top of the soft cushion of human bodies. His torso bounced gently, loosening the grip of the sword. His hands flopped to his sides. His eyes staring into oblivion.

18

The atmosphere was sombre. The air smelled of ripped fresh flesh and sweat. The floor carpeted with dead and dying bodies. To Donald, however, it was nothing new. Looking at the bodies lying at his feet, images of 1910 flashed in his mind as if it were yesterday. He had come to know each and every one of the villagers and they him. He had lived in their homes, eaten their food and slept in their beds, and yet, killed almost every last one of them. He did not experience guilt or torment for what he had done, only desire to be free. He would do anything to enable that goal to be achieved. They had given up all rights to their lives when they had signed on the line. Their souls were his to command, and there was nothing, anyone could do about it. Not even *him*.

He cursed the human spirit and their insatiable capacity to stay alive at all costs. It had been one such human who had taken the step to flee the village that had brought him where he was today. She *will* pay. "No longer will I be condemned to hell. No longer will I be a puppet to your will and desires. No longer will you control these people, and they bow down to you They will all bow down to ME!"

His anger exploded and echoed throughout the entire school. Books on shelves, chairs on tables, anything not secure fell to the floor, windows smashed, and walls cracked. His voice extended beyond the village and reverberated through the very mountains themselves.

Donald listened to the dying echoes, cherishing their massacring memory; then flicking his cloak arrogantly, he returned to Mary. She lay motionless on the stone altar in her white dress. Her arms strapped to the stone with leather straps that sprouted from the marble itself wrapping around her wrists like chocking weeds. Blood stained the ends of her sleeves where she had struggled to loosen the grip, and dirt smeared the lower part of the dress. Her bare feet covered in dust from the stone floor.

Donald smiled, at last, his moment was about to happen. He did not care that midnight had come and gone, that was just a ploy to intensify the moment for his followers. He knew humanity's relentless desire for entertainment and thrill was what really drove these pitiful creatures. It did not take him long to discover this to be their strongest weakness; they simply bowed to his will. The truth was, he did not even need those villagers. He had only resurrected them to authenticate this village to get her here. The school was just a means to an end; a calculated manoeuvre to encourage the descendant of Rose McFadgen to return to Kirkfale. He could have gone anywhere in the world, to any shoemaker, but he wanted revenge. He wanted Rose and her descendants to pay for *her* foolishness. That was why he had waited one hundred years, and that is why he had restored Kirkfale. It was all perfectly planned to every minute detail. Everything was supposed to happen according to HIS will.

Donald glanced back at the body of Iain; still lying sprawled over others with the sword protruding from his chest. The red ruby at the base of the hilt reflected what little light hit it from the burning torches, giving it a reddish glow, whilst the blade had a whitish haze about it. Donald did not really care, even when a flash of light rippled the length of the blade. He assumed it was just a reflective trick. The room was dim where Iain lay and every flicker of a shadow against the cold metal was magnified a thousand times. He cursed their free-will and remembered when they were given it; even *then* he thought it was a bad idea.

As one of *his* generals, he believed giving humans free will would make them powerful, too powerful. Being able to think made them a liability ensuring they never did what they were expected to do. None of them were controllable; a fact he proved in the garden. "Still," he reminded himself, "I have used their ability to choose their own way many times throughout history. If they are doing what they want, feeding their own desires, glorifying themselves, then they are not doing what *he* wants." The hatred for the one he once loved manifested as a growl, "You will pay for my incarceration." He bellowed waving a clenched fist to the ceiling.

Turning back to the body that lay on the altar, he wondered if he had been heard. He was all-seeing, all-knowing, ever-present after all, but he still wondered if he was bothered that the one, he exiled from Heaven was about to be set free. Donald smiled. His plan was flawless. His plan, even after the numerous complications that had postponed the inevitable, *would* succeed. He will roam the world fully disguised, totally undetectable, building his army against the one who abandoned him here for all eternity. He knew, of course, an end will come. That was certain. But, until that time, he would gather as many of his puny humans and turn them against him. In the end, there will be no one to worship him, no matter how big and almighty he is.

At least, that had been in his plan ever since the garden.

His influence was taking hold. The world was turning anti-Christian, which meant, anti-Christ. People questioning their beliefs. Brothers against brothers. Parents against children. Countries against countries. Man's greed and sexual desires were among the strongest emotions. They were beginning to realise who really had the power. The abuse of his gifts. Aggressive natures. Inherent desires and willingness to cause harm to others. Their lies. Their adultery. Theft. Murder. Prostitution. Love of money. Their insatiable appetite to want ever more.

His presence on Earth was rampant, but, to him, it was not enough. His power over most was only short-lived. He could not stay on Earth for too long in one go, he kept getting recognised because of his cloven feet. His feet. The only part of him humans recognised. Even those who had done everything against their creator, even they knew what his cloven feet meant. Many ran in terror, but most called out who he was. You would think, an ancient, all powerful being such as he, would know how to cover his feet, disguise them from everyone. You would think that God would give him that skill. Perhaps that was his plan, all along. To limit his power. A weakness to prevent him garnering too much power.

A weakness he will correct now.

He took the dagger resting on the stone altar to the side of Mary's hand and grasping it firmly. As he raised it unnecessarily high above his head, his excitement electrified. His plans were about to be completed; he was about to be set free. He was so focused that everything, other than the key to freedom before him on the altar, was a distant blur. They meant absolutely nothing to him now. Nothing could stop him, not even the Father.

He did not see the blood smeared on the blade of his sword gather together as though drawn by a magnet. He missed it as it trickled down into the body of Iain. He was completely oblivious to the light emanating from the blood as it entered the wound and began a healing process. His focus on Mary, meant that he missed the white light engulfing Iain's entire lifeless body.

He did not, however, miss the familiar feeling of a presence he had not felt in such a long time. A presence that filled a gaping hole he had been forced to suffer since his exile.

He already knew who stood behind him, but a sense of belonging, that even angels feel, urged him to turn.

19

"Michael," Donald said as he came face to face with the one being that could stop him from achieving his destiny, the only one who could send him back to hell, the Archangel Michael. Although Donald saw the body of Iain animated before him, he knew the presence within, the spirit inside the body was that of one of the most powerful angels in God's legions.

He was not worried in the slightest, however, but did have a quizzical look. His right eyebrow rose slightly and his left lowered, he tilted his head a fraction from the norm, and his bottom lip crumpled up as the top lip stretched over it. The dagger still held within his hand felt warm. He had concealed the dagger behind his cloak, where he also kept his right hand poised to thrust if the need came to it. Stepping down from the platform, he faced the new arrival. The sacrifice would have to wait. The corner of his mouth curled ever so slightly at the memory of his effective lie, but it quickly disappeared as he watched his brother, Michael survey the sword he now held. *His* sword.

The sword bore many memories for Donald, particularly during the massacre of 1910 in the very location he stood. He had used that sword for many centuries, right enough, in fact it was a remnant of a time long since gone, crafted with the most precious of metal. Now, the Archangel, Michael held it in his right hand. He could not help but notice the whitish glow about the blade giving it an aura and making the pattern more three-dimensional. A part of him yearned to hold the sword again, it had been a part of him for so long. It had not escaped his attention that if it came to a fight, his significantly smaller knife compared to Michael's glowing sword would be no match.

Donald watched his fellow angel look slowly around at the carpet of bodies at their feet. He looked as if he had no recollection of what had happened. Finally, Michael walked around turning faces with the end of his sword. A strange behaviour thought Donald, but he said nothing. He knew better. He wondered what his brother was thinking when he stopped at Andrew's body, the traitor, the infiltrator, the one sent to spy on Donald's activities. Michael placed the tip of the sword on Andrew's chest, where the exit wound was and lowered his head as if to mourn a friend. Although something Donald had not seen in a long time, it was not unexpected. After a moment longer, he looked up and Donald noticed the glisten of a tear just to the side of his nose but ignored it. "To what do I owe this pleasure, Brother?" He said finally. His voice low, controlled, but powerful.

Michael did not answer immediately but continued looking at Donald as if to read his mind or something similar. He pulled the sword from Andrew's chest and brought it up to stand next to his leg; the tip finding an opening in the carpet of bodies. In fact, Donald noticed for the first time, Michael was not standing on *any* bodies as he had moments before, but on a clearing between bodies. "Our Father has sent me."

Donald smirked; he had thought as much, why else would an archangel be here. Perhaps, he had touched a raw nerve in his Father's heart. He wondered if his attempts to walk the Earth would get his Father's attention, but until now, he had not made any effort to stop him. "I think you and Father are mistaken; it is not the right time."

Michael did not move from his stance, "No, it is not the time for us to do battle, but it IS time for you to stop what you are doing here."

"Why?" Donald was frustrated; his eyes narrowed, and his eyebrows lowered. He managed to keep his anger in check, but still raised his free hand for emphasis, "Why can I not walk the Earth?"

"You know the answer to that," Michael betrayed no emotion at all.

"I did it all for HIM," Donald lied. He was referring to an incident that occurred so many centuries ago that resulted in him being forced from his home, the only place he loved. He had been exiled from Heaven and damned for all eternity.

"You always were a good liar, Brother."

Donald could have exploded at that moment, but figured it was pointless, since it WAS the truth. He was named the Prince of Lies, after all. He had encouraged so many humans to lie and cheat and had laughed at the consequences. "Creation would be boring if *everyone* told the truth *all* the time."

Michael did not show any sign of amusement. His stare had not altered since he first spoke, "Your influence on mankind will come to an end."

"What do you mean 'will', my influence on man is only short lived, why do you think I work so hard?" Donald raised his voice; he could feel the blood rush to his cheeks and neck with anger; a human response. He mentally cursed his body. He willed the calmness to return. Anger would solve nothing. "You still have not answered my question."

"Our Father sent me to remind you that you are forbidden to directly kill any of His creation."

"Oh! I'm forbidden to kill any of HIS creation." Donald mocked, shaking his head slightly, "I will take her soul and roam this world undetected." He motioned to the lifeless body on the stone table.

"Do you really think our Father will allow that to happen?"

"Come on Michael, our Father has forgotten what it is like down here. Man has lost hope in their creator. Our Father is always the last thing on their mind. Even their governments are run on greed and deception. Their pride has forced their sons and daughters to fight wars they do not agree with. Hatred and misguided instruction have killed millions for the sake of God. Out of all creation, mankind are the only ones that prey, hunt, kill, and eat their own kind."

Michael remained silent for a short moment. Donald tried to ascertain what his brother was thinking, but, his thoughts were his own and he betrayed no emotion. "Our Father did not make 'automatons' just to worship; He wanted them to freely choose to love Him."

"And look where that has got them. They need *me*. They lack direction and leadership. They need someone to look up to, someone who will care for them," Donald pleaded. He knew it was only a matter of time before he would succeed, after all, it was written he would be set free eventually, he just wanted to do it on his own terms. Of course, he also knew his Son would return again to put him into the abyss, but he wanted to create as much discord as he could before that day arrived.

"Man has fallen far from grace that is true, but our Father has planned it all, and it will go according to HIS will and design, not yours, not mine, not anyone else's but His." Michael looked round at the bodies again, "Your endeavours here will inevitably fail as they always have, brother."

Donald's frustration was growing exponentially. He turned back towards the altar where the sacrifice was still lying. The dagger was still in his hand hiding between the folds of his black robe. He only needed to make one step and thrust it into her chest and her soul would escape, enter into him, and it would all be over. He would be set free. Free to wander the world undetected and build an army that will overthrow even the angels. However, as if Michael heard his thoughts, he stepped closer allowing the tip of the sword to tap on the stone floor.

"Brother, end this now, if you do not it will end in your own humiliation. All creation will see you for the fraud you are, they will see right through your plans and push you away. If you stop now and wait for the right time to be set free, you will have your chance." Michael was not going to take 'no' for an answer.

Donald snapped round, "I know what is written in Revelations, just as well as you do, Brother. I know He will rule for a thousand years after which I will be free for a short time before being thrown into the eternal abyss. I'd rather take my chances now."

Michael looked at his brother for a moment, "You chose your path, now you must follow it. You have been warned." With that, Michael lifted the sword and thrust it downwards where it made a clang, sending sparks in every direction. Donald watched as Iain's body fell limply onto the floor. He smiled. That familiar feeling was gone in an instant.

He walked over to Iain's body and nudged him with his foot, just to check his brother had actually left the human's body. He kicked the body more forcibly, smiling with each kick. He felt a sense of achievement and pride knowing he had finally won. He kicked again and watched as Iain's body rolled backwards, the sword was nowhere to be seen, at least, Donald could not see it.

He returned to the altar and took up position. Nobody could stop him now. He closed his eyes to quieten his mind and took a few deep breaths to steady his heart. Even though he used to be a divine being, he still experienced the same emotional states as humans that walked the Earth, albeit at a higher level.

Opening his eyes, he took hold of the dagger once more with both hands and raised it above his head, "Now is the time, no one can stop me!"

"You've got that wrong!" A voice that Black Donald had thought he would never hear again cut through the air, and he felt the cold sting of a sharp blade slash across his back.

20

Iain did not understand how he was now standing without any blood-stained clothing or pains and aches from the fight, or why he was now holding Black Donald's sword. However, he DID remember a lot of what had happened, although he could not explain it. He had these memories he did not remember experiencing, a conversation in this very location with Donald. Iain recalled many episodes of déjà vous throughout his life, but this was the only time it had been so clear and so real. He had no recollection of having the conversation with Donald, yet he could vividly remember nearly every single word spoken. Strangest of all, he could 'see' in his mind's eye, the true image of the one who stood before him now, yet with his true eyes he only saw the headmaster and Mayor of Kirkfale, also called Black Donald. He also could not begin to fathom how he saw Donald as an almighty being capable of smiting him with a thought. A part of him found it hard to believe, that this frail-looking man could be, anyone other than this frail old man. Seconds ago, a word had flashed in his mind many times, but it was now a distant echo. However, he knew, somehow, that it was the true name of the beast that stood just a few feet away from him.

The headmaster stepped down from the platform again, but this time approached Iain. Anger was clear on his face, yet the rest of his body seemed expertly restrained. Iain noticed the fruits of his labour when a small section of Donald's robe fell away from the bottom hem.

He spotted the dagger in Donald's right hand. His arm was straight down in line with the torso of his body. Although he knew he was no match for a being with celestial strength, he was confident he could hold his own with the sword he now pointed towards the oncoming frail old man.

His foot moved back and kicked something, making him take his eyes off Donald for a moment to see what it was. Vomit welled up in his stomach when he saw a dead body lying in a pool of blood that he had caused. He forced himself to push the bile down and refocused. Now was not time to feel guilt for murder. He gulped as Donald took another step closer. He tried not to show his knees were trembling, he was glad his legs were apart; otherwise, he was sure the knees would knock each other.

Donald swung his arm holding the dagger to the side and then swiftly towards the sword. It clanged upon impact and pushed the sword away. Iain pushed all his energy into his arms and swung the sword to meet another offensive swing from Donald. With another clang, Iain was sure the dagger's blade had grown a few inches in length. Again, both swung, and the blades met with a clash. As Donald swung his arm, his other arm swung the other direction to counterbalance his thrust. Iain, however, kept his stance reasonably still, maintaining a strong barrier against the attacks.

After several more swings of the dagger, Donald stopped, perhaps he felt it was pointless to continue, Iain could not be sure. Iain spotted his avenue to Mary and began taking small steps towards the altar. He needed to get between the altar and Donald, but that would be difficult, particularly since Donald had spotted the opening and was already moving to block his advances. Donald turned and outstretched his free arm towards Andrew's dead body and immediately a scrape echoed throughout the room. Iain watched as another sword, similar to the one he held now flew up into the air, twirled so that the hilt faced Donald and zoomed into his awaiting hand. Iain swallowed hard.

He took a deep breath and released it slowly whilst he waited for Donald to attack again; He pounced onto Iain with both dagger and sword swirling in several different circular patterns. It was all Iain could do to remain on his feet. He moved faster than he had ever moved before and made contact with each and every slice of sword, dagger, or both. Donald was relentless with his attacks and betrayed no evidence that he was tiring. His chest seemed to rise and fall at the normal speed.

Continuing his advance, Donald forced Iain to retreat. Iain still matching every swiping attack by Donald. He hoped Donald was becoming more frustrated which led to being more forgetful, allowing him to edge closer to Mary. Now looking into the eyes of the evil Mayor of Kirkfale, Iain only saw blind fury.

Swinging both blades, Donald caught Iain's sword as he followed through with a defensive move. For a moment, Iain struggled to withdraw his sword, so much so, he missed Donald's foot kicking him in the gut and sending him back into a stone column. Somehow, he managed to keep hold of the sword even as he crashed to the hard floor.

Rolling to a kneeling position, Iain ducked just in time as Donald swung his sword again. He thrust his own sword whilst he crouched, but the blade was pushed away with Donald's dagger. "Why won't you just die, already!" Donald bellowed through another attack.

Iain tried to think of a comeback. Nothing came to mind. Instead, he rolled to the side, dodging a downward thrust of Donald's sword, jumped to his feet and readied himself for when Donald attacked again. He felt like he had a renewed strength well up inside but knew that was impossible. Donald swung and Iain blocked and kicked his leg up. Donald staggered back slightly. He made the split decision to continue attacking, whilst he had the advantage and swung his sword at the chest, but as expected, Donald blocked with his dagger. Iain twirled round and swung in one smooth motion. His sword was an extension of his arm. His fencing training taking control. This time he struck at the other side. The attack was blocked by Donald's sword. Iain immediately twirled into another similar manoeuvre but lowered his sword. His blade followed a downward diagonal direction.

His calculation was spot on, and the sword made contact with Donald's ripped robe. The sword got caught in the fabric, pulled with all his might creating a satisfying rip. Donald retaliated by swooping HIS sword and smashing Iain's sword away, clear of the material, he followed the swoop with an elbow to Iain's face destabilising him. With one further step forward, Donald thrust the dagger into Iain's side below his ribs. Grabbing the dagger, Iain stumbled backwards and felt the warm, wet blood seep through his fingers, again.

Inspecting the wound, Iain quietly took a moment to catch his breath and hoping the dagger had not hit any major arteries. Despite the pain and the blood staining his hands and clothes, Iain forced himself to ignore it. Looking up at Donald, he was surprised he just stood watching him with his narrowed eyes. Taking hold of the dagger, Iain clenched his teeth and pulled.

"Arrrrgh!" The excruciating pain ripped through his torso. White explosions like mini fireworks flashed in his eyelids. He allowed the surge of agony to subside to a bearable level before throwing the bloodied dagger behind the altar. He slowly stood, grabbing his sword from the stone floor. All the while, he maintained eye-contact with Donald, who showed no sign of exhaustion, but stood allowing his sword to hang by his side.

He felt a movement behind him. Turning his head, he realised Mary was stirring. Somewhere in the fight, he had managed to make his way to the altar. MARY. Mustering strength, Iain swung his sword over his head and brought it down on the leather straps holding Mary's wrists.

"STOP!" Donald demanded.

Iain snapped back and felt a pain in his side, which quickly died down, just as quickly as it appeared. He was just in time to see Donald swing his sword with both his hands and growling like a wild bear. Within seconds, he had crossed the room and was slicing down at Iain. Dodging to the left, Iain heard the sword crash into the stone altar, the echo bounced off the walls. He snapped round to see if Mary was hurt and smiled when she had rolled to the other side of the altar. Her screams were ear-piercing, but he had to block them out in order to save her.

"Hey Donald," he called. Donald through his rage, snapped around. His teeth were clenched. Foam coming from his lips. His eyes were glowing amber embers and his skin was redder than Iain remembered. "I know who you are!" he teased.

21

Mary fumbled at the leather strap securing her left wrist. She forced herself to ignore the pain pulsating in both of her hands. She had just narrowly missed the Mayor smash a sword down against the altar she had been, only moments earlier, securely fastened to. She could not understand why the Mayor of Kirkfale had strapped her to a stone table, or why he was now fighting her husband with swords, of all things. She had to free the band around her left wrist before the Mayor attacked her again, but her strength was waning, her nails were broken, and blood oozed from the fingertips. Her wrists were red raw and blistered. The lace from her sleeves stuck to her skin in the seeping blood. Then she stopped struggling; her strength all gone. She rested her head on the stone slab, defeated, its coldness provided a momentary distraction. Behind her, she could still hear the grunts and clangs.

    She wanted to peer over and see what was happening, but she was gripped in fear. The last thing she wanted was to watch Iain die, she loved him too much. Guilt started to well up. Guilt for dragging Iain up to the place. If she had not jumped at the opportunity to set up her business, she was confident they would not now be fighting to survive.

She spotted a glint of light; it looked like a dagger and reaching her hand out she realised it was too far out. Sighing, she closed her eyes knowing what she must do.

One, two, three…

She jerked toward the dagger and felt a clunk in her shoulder. She screamed. Wincing with pain, she hoped it did not attract any unwanted attention. When the pain became bearable, she reached for the dagger once again.

Eventually, her hand came across the dagger's handle, and she grabbed it as quietly and quickly as possible. Bringing the dagger round, she reached up to her bound wrist and began moving the blade back and forth as if it was a saw. Slowly, the dagger began cutting through the leather.

22

Iain stood again after being knocked down for the umpteenth time. A quick glimpse over to the altar confirmed that Mary was gone, where to, he could only guess. He wiped a drip of blood from his lower lip and picked up his sword that had been knocked from his hand, again. He turned back to Donald, who still revealed no sign of any exhaustion, whereas Iain was way past that stage. He got to his knees and then to his feet using the sword as a support.

Donald held his sword down with the tip touching the floor; his free arm hung down by his side. To Iain, it seemed that all the wounds he had inflicted on Donald were non-existent; there was no sign of any injury anywhere on his body. Sure, the robe had been ripped in a random pattern of straight lines, but there was no blood.

Moments later, Donald lifted his sword and sprung forward, Iain did likewise to counteract his attack. Their swords clashed in another ferocious volley and with each contact Iain felt his strength wavering even more. He had to think of something fast, because he could not keep this up for much longer. He knew he should not have tried bluffing

Donald when he lied about knowing who he was, but at least he got his attention away from Mary, and now she appeared to be free and away from the danger. Something inside him smiled, but he could not allow it to distract him.

Another clang and Iain were forced down to his knees. He wanted to stand back up, but every inch of his body cried out in exhaustion. He glimpsed at the altar and spotted Mary's head bob up and for a split second their eyes met. She was scared. He was scared. But in that brief exchange, as he looked into her deep brown eyes, his heart melted just like the day they first met. They both knew, whatever happened now, they were in this together, as they had always been.

He shook his head, wiped sweat from his brow and rubbed his eyes. It felt like he had been at this for hours. Perhaps he had. At least, with Mary out of the Donald's immediate focus, she had a chance. He refocused on Donald who, once again, was charging with his sword raised. Grabbing his sword with both hands, he mirrored Donald's charge. He took a deep breath and began crying out at the top of his voice.

Donald swung hard. The swords chimed and Iain lost grip of his own sword. It went flying across the room, where it crashed into the far wall. Pain surged through his hands. His knuckles ached. His strength was depleted. He was exhausted. All he could do was watch Donald recover from the swing and decide what to do with him. He allowed his arms to fall helplessly to his sides. He fell to his knees. Pain stung his kneecaps. His head pounded in agony as if Donald was knocking him with a mallet. His eyes burning like fire. His mouth dry as a desert. His heart ached for his love. Sweat and blood matted his hair.

His clothes covered in thick red ooze. He yearned for the end.

Mary's head bobbed back up from her hiding place. Iain found a renewed sense of determination. He tried to stir up more energy through his anger but failed. Just as he yearned for more strength, Donald spoke, "I will not kill you, today. You may still prove useful in the coming days when I rule the Earth." His voice was deep and low, totally unrecognisable from the headmaster's.

Iain felt it pierce his mind as easily a knife through soft butter. It made him cringe. He wanted to grab Donald's voice box and rip it out. Fantasy. He had no strength to even lift his arms. He was defeated. May was defeated. He had allowed Mary to be killed. "But for now..." Iain felt Donald's clenched fist smash against his head like a bulldozer hitting a wall.

His body flew through the air and landed on top of several bodies. Raising his head, he looked around, for what use it would do him. The sword lay on the stone floor, plastered in blood, not too far from him, but just outside his reach. He had exhausted all his resources for strength preventing him from moving closer. He felt so tired. He fought his eyelids from closing. They were so heavy. He used his last ounce of strength to keep them open. Mary was his only thought. How he had let her down. He was about to lose her forever, and there was nothing he could do about it.

Donald turned back to the stone altar, already realising she was gone and hiding behind the table. Iain tried to find the strength to chase him, or even to shout out, but nothing came. His chest heaved. Every breath a sting of agony. The sword just out of reach. The stench of decaying flesh filled his nostrils, urging him to vomit. He tried, desperately to move. The connection between his brain and muscles seemed non-existent.

All he could do was watch helplessly as Donald moved ever closer to the stone tablet and to Mary. Within seconds, he succumbed to the powerful urge to close his eyes.

23

It had been some time since Mary had last heard something from the other side of the altar, and she hoped that meant good news. She sat with her knees bent up and her arms clasped round them rocking back and forward. Streams of tears poured out of her eyes, yet she forced herself to be silent. The last thing she needed was to be found, it was not the best location to hide, but for now, it was all she had. She glanced to her right; the dagger laid where she had left it. She grabbed it without making a sound.

She brushed her finger over her wet cheek and moved her matted hair back from her eye. A slight pain shot through her wrist; she rubbed it; but it did not sooth it. Closing her eyes, she rested her head on the stone slab again. Her thoughts were filled of Iain, of their life before Kirkfale and why they had to come here. The guilt was paramount. She banged her head against the stone. If Iain was lying dead now, she would never forgive herself. Opening her eyes, she looked at the dagger and movement in the shiny blade grabbed her attention.

Her sore wrist was yanked almost pulling her other shoulder out of its socket. She looked up and screamed. A figure with red burning eyes pulling her over the table with ease stood before her. She tried to struggle but he was too strong. He snarled and grabbed her other arm and thrust her on to the stone slab. She squealed in pain and tried to wriggle free, but his grip was just too powerful for her. She shrieked, "Iain!"

"He cannot help you now." The Mayor's lips moved, but Mary heard the words in her mind. He smiled, "Look, he lies with the rest of the dead." His other hand extended behind him.

Mary felt the blood drain from her face and screamed, "Iain, Iain, wake up." She struggled against the Mayor's powerful grip, "Iain, you can't be dead, I need you." Iain did not move. Not even a flicker.

"And now, Mary McFadgen, I have waited for this moment ever since your ancestor fled me one hundred years ago." He forcibly bound her wrists again.

"McFadgen? Who's that? What are you talking about? Wh…who are you?" She struggled against the constraints again, but they were much tighter than before. Giving in, she looked up at the sneering face of the Mayor. She felt a weird sensation behind her eyes, a burning. She wanted to turn away, but something stopped. An unseen force. Something powerful. She could not resist. Her eyes fixed upon those deep, red eyes looking down at her. The image of a demon flashed in her mind. No, not just *any* demon; *the* demon.

"Finally, Mary, you are fortunate to be witness to my rebirth," he raised the dagger, she had not seen him pick up, "Once your soul is mine, Mary McFadgen, the debt your ancestor created one hundred years ago will be paid in full and I will be free to roam *my* kingdom."

She screamed.

*

The darkness was restful. The quietness peaceful. Iain just wanted to lie there for as long as he could. He had to recover completely in order to finish off Donald and the only way to do that was to linger in that place of total tranquillity. But there was something not right, something that did not sit well with him, even in that soporific state. His thoughts were of Mary, her need and how she could not stand up against the power of Donald. He yearned to wake up, rush to her side, and save her from death. He wanted to get up on his feet and stab Donald in the heart, assuming he had one. He wanted to...

"What you want is not important, what HE wants is all you need." Iain opened his eyes and saw a man walking towards him. He blinked and then blinked again, just to be sure. The entire chamber had disappeared in favour of whiteness, no other description was apt. For the first time he felt revitalised, his strength returned, his exhaustion gone, even his clothes were whole again. The man took Iain's hand and as if his eyes had suddenly been opened, he recognised the man as his dead friend, Andrew. Feeling relaxed, all his troubles had just drifted away.

"Am I dead?" Andrew smiled.

His white suit reflected the brilliance from the surrounding whiteness. His cheek bones became more prominent as the corners of his mouth curved up. A twinkle in his eye seemed to put Iain at ease, "No, you are not dead. I am God's messenger."

"His messenger?" Iain looked around, just to check he had not missed anything about the scenery. It was still white. All of it. He could not quite believe his eyes. "Is this Heaven?"

The messenger smiled again, "No, this is not Heaven, you are not dead, you just need a nudge, and I am here to do just that." He guided Iain forward and they walked, amongst the vast whiteness that was like an undecorated room; a blank canvass, "My Father knew this would all happen, it was all part of His plan."

"You mean, us coming to Kirkfale, Donald giving me a job and then taking it away from me, kidnapping Mary, and then bringing me here?" Andrew nodded with each example.

"It's all part of His divine plan. You see, Iain, there is a reason for everything that happens; you were chosen by God before you were born. Chosen for this specific purpose." He stopped and turned Iain to face him, "You," he said pointing, "must recognise Black Donald for who he really is and stop him roaming Earth."

"Mary?" Iain suddenly remembered.

"Is fine, as long as you reveal Black Donald's true identity," he said.

Iain turned and took a couple steps away from his friend, Andrew, "But, who *is* this Black Donald?" he uttered throwing his hands up in frustration.

"You have all that you need to fulfil His will for your life." The voice sounded quieter. Iain turned to find he was along again. He blinked, trying to understand what he had just heard. This all sounded too far-fetched, like a story out of a book, but there was something familiar about it all, something…he just could not put his finger on it. Then the darkness engulfed him, and he felt a sudden rushing sensation as though being pulled backwards at great speed.

When he opened his eyes and saw the chamber again, the dimly lit candles, by comparison to where he had just been, gave the room a darker feel than he remembered, but he had to ignore it and move. Lifting his head, he looked over to the altar and saw Donald holding the dagger above his head again, and panic struck him. Was he too late? He stood as quickly and quietly as possible, and thought about getting his sword, but then something inside him told him it would be unnecessary. "*You have all that you need to fulfil his will for your life. He won't give you anything you cannot handle.*"

As if an opaque veil had been lifted from his eyes, Iain noticed the red feet at the base of the black robe worn by Donald. He had not seen them before but knew exactly what they were. It looked odd, but also fitting for whom they belonged to. Everything was now clear in his mind, and he knew exactly what to do.

He rose and stepped forward, "Black Donald, I command you to leave this place." For a moment there was no response, but then a gurgling sound filled the chamber, or was it laughter? Iain assumed the latter. Donald slowly lowered the dagger to his side and turned around, fixing his fiery, red eyes firmly on Iain. Iain gasped but held his stance. He was not expecting demonic eyes. It just confirmed what he now knew, what he expected all along, actually.

"YOU, command ME?" Donald's voice was almost playful. A shiver zapped down Iain's spine, but he resisted the urge to shake in response. "You have no power over me, I am a god compared to you. I should have killed you when I had the chance."

Iain noticed Donald had brought the dagger into full view, "And now it would seem another opportunity has presented itself."

Iain smiled, even though he did not feel like doing it, "You are a 'god' who is trapped."

"You pathetic fool; you cannot possibly comprehend what or who you are dealing with."

"Actually, I know more than you think, Satan!" Iain felt a little pride in his answer, "Your cloven feet are a dead giveaway…"

"WHAT?" Within moments, the entire room shook violently. Standing stone slabs, smashing into smaller fragments and Iain almost stumbled but managed to steady himself against a stable stone column. Donald exploded in rage and fire, "NOOOOOOOOOoooooooo!" His body erupted in red and orange embers being sent in every direction like a large firework. Iain ducked below a flare heading towards him and as he did so, he heard a loud roar echoing from every direction.

It only lasted a few seconds before the roar faded and the chamber fell silent and darker. A few embers from scraps of material were scattered about the altar. After allowing his eyes to adjust to the lower level of light, Iain approached Mary and placed his hand on her cheek. She slowly opened her eyes, and his heart began beating faster. "Hey, you," he said as he began loosening the straps holding her wrists.

Mary smiled, "Hey you, is it over?" She looked exhausted through her tears. Iain began cutting through the leather straps and nodded.

"I hope so." He leaned closer after freeing her arms. Mary put her arms round her husband and kissed him. As their lips parted, the room began shaking again, Mary tightened her hold and Iain looked round, "Come on, we've got to get out here, now!"

24

The violent shudders reminded Iain of an earthquake, or at least what he thought was an earthquake, having never witnessed one before. With one arm around Mary's waist guiding her along the corridor, Iain dared not look back, but guessed the building was falling down around them. The statues that lined the corridor toppled as they approached, as if a hidden force pushed them purposely off their plinths in front of them. Paintings that were secure to the walls fell and smashed, narrowly missing the escapees. Then there was that roar; deep, loud, and amplifying with each step closer to the main school door. He wondered if they would actually escape in one piece but could not let that stop him. Mary must get out at all costs, even if he had to sacrifice himself, such was his love for her. He hoped it would not come to that, but if it did, he was prepared.

As the staircase loomed ever closer, the noise of exploding walls and floor tiles became deafening. To Iain, it felt like he was in one of those action movies he used to watch as a teenager, where he had to escape from the claws of death before time ran out, only this was real, and he *did* have to escape before they were killed by the devil, himself.

"You cannot escape, there is no place you can run from me," snarled Satan from everywhere. Iain tried to blot the voice out, the last thing he needed was to be stopped when they were so close to the door. He was hoping that would end it all, but there was something niggling in the back of his head, and he just could not put his finger on it.

Iain pushed Mary just as a large section of the ceiling crashed to the floor; he managed to jump out of its path just in time as it exploded into smaller pieces, sending shards in every direction. He said a silent prayer, jumped the rubble, and grabbed Mary. He was right; the school was crumbling around them. They did not have much time.

"Her soul will be mine!" Iain ignored the threat and guided Mary through the fallen and falling debris.

At the bottom of the last staircase, he felt a sense of achievement and joy, but it was short-lived when the door slammed shut, "Do you honestly think I would let you just walk out the door." He turned to where he thought the voice came from, but there was no one there. Instead, he continued towards the door with Mary, hoping an idea would pop into his head.

"It won't budge," cried Iain tugging desperately at the handle. Mary hung her arms limply by her sides and began to sob. "Listen to me, we are going to get out of here, you understand me?" said Iain as he put his arms around her, protecting her from the falling rocks and splinters.

"My power is supreme; you are nothing to me. I will have your soul, both of them."

"I'd give anything for him to shut up right now!" Iain looked for options, there were too few to count. He held Mary closer; he felt her body warmth and the occasional jump as she sobbed into his shoulder. He watched as more of the ceiling and walls fell to the floor, opening holes for daylight to pass through. Rain from the heavy grey clouds began wetting the floor and the debris that littered it.

Iain snapped around when an explosion blew the staircase out, at least Mary would be safe from the blast and debris. He felt every single sting of rubble hitting his back; it was agonising, but for Mary, he would bear it, even as blood began seeping onto his shirt from each impact. An explosion of fire forced them against the door. Their bodies fell to the floor. Looking up, Iain saw flames reaching out in every direction, and at the heart of them all, a figure.

Standing on two cloven hooves, the hideous creature snarled at Iain. He made a sound that was almost a laugh, "Time's up! You've nowhere to run." He raised his hand, and fire shot out towards Iain and Mary, just as the large door exploded inwards deflecting the flames. Iain looked back towards the opened door and saw two humans standing with a brilliant white aura flowing from them. Iain felt a sense of relief wash over him when he recognised the old lady and police officer he had run into on his way to the school.

"Lucifer, you have lost, leave now or be sent to the abyss before the allotted time." The voice of the police officer, bold and loud shouted as he stepped onto the broken door. The old lady looked in Iain's direction and nodded, "Hurry, get beyond the village boundary," her voice was focused and calm, "we will hold him off."

"Who are you people?" Iain was shocked to say the least, but stood, nonetheless. Mary did not, however. Iain picked her up and carried her. She had been knocked out when they were thrown to the floor following the first explosion.

"You dare enter my presence and make demands of me?" The one they called Lucifer spoke to the new arrivals, "You have no authority."

"I come in our Father's name, you will return to hell, or we will vanquish you to the abyss." Lucifer laughed.

"That is not for you to decide or perform."

"No, but I will do it anyway." Iain could not believe his ears. Was this policeman an angel? How did they know each other? Although it seemed outrageous, it sounded right, why wouldn't there be angels when Lucifer's here? "You will leave this place," the old woman repeated with just as much power in her voice as the policeman's. Iain looked at them and then back to Lucifer. The beast stood at least double the height of the policeman and at first glance, it was not a fair fight, but that was not his concern. He had to get Mary out. He moved quickly towards the open door stopping on the threshold. He looked at his two allies before continuing through the door, "The engines on, the road is clear, get beyond the border." The woman motioned towards the police car that was facing the door. The policeman continued to confront Satan.

"What about you?" Iain was not about to let someone die for him.

"We will be able to hold Lucifer just enough time for you to escape. He doesn't have any *real* power anyway." She smiled before turning back to Lucifer and deflecting another shot of fire. Iain did not stay any longer and headed towards the car. He put Mary into the passenger seat before climbing into the driver's seat. Lingering just enough time to see the policemen hit by fire and the woman retaliating with a white bolt in response, Iain put the car into reverse and spun it around. He took one more look in the rear-view mirror before slamming his foot on the accelerator.

*

As Iain glanced into his rear-view mirror, he saw the ground begin to crack and fire grow out from beneath the surface. If he were not already going as fast as he could, he would have increased his speed. The gorge seemed to be following the car as he drove down the main high street of Kirkfale, heading out of the village.

Only a few more minutes! He gave a quick glance over to Mary, she was still. For a split moment, the worst crossed his mind, and he was about to slam the brakes on. A sharp intake of air as she turned her head, confirmed she was only asleep. A sense of relief shrouded him like the feeling of cool, fresh air in the morning.

An exploding building on the side of the road refocused Iain allowing him to swerve away from falling debris. The ground itself crumbled as the gaping chasm reached the back of the car, but that was not going to stop Iain. He had not come this far to lose it this close to the end. The clouds above unleashed their barrage of water and hail upon the road, but Iain drove regardless. Nothing was going to stop him now, nothing.

He passed the final building, the burnt-out shop of Mary's shoe-making business and the reason they both dropped everything and moved to Scotland. He knew the border of the village of Kirkfale was not far away. They were going to make it. Iain looked at the reflection of everything behind and could not see the start of the quake. That meant it was under the car.

He rounded the corner and crossed the village boundary line and finally the shaking stopped. The cracked halted in its pursuit, and everything returned to normal. The clouds disappeared and the sun shone, giving the countryside a glorious feel to it, as if summer had suddenly appeared. He wanted to stop the car and look back at the location of where Kirkfale was being laid wasted. He looked at Sleeping Beauty sat in the passenger's seat, stopping was not an option for him. Instead, he continued driving forward, leaving Kirkfale to the history books, without looking back.

25

Standing at the border of where a once thriving community village stopped, a lone uniformed figure watched the shrinking rear of the car escaping the grasps of Lucifer. The turmoil had calmed, and the stress gone, all that was left of Kirkfale were many piles of rocks, bricks, and wood. Despite this, the lone figure just stood watching the car, as if to check the car and its contents had escaped. He smiled and was joined by two other figures.

For a moment, all three continued to stare at the road, even though the car had disappeared over the horizon seconds before. The glorious view of the Father's providential grace and love for his creation. Birds were flying over the mountains, sheep and cows happily grazing in the fields that lined the road. The waterfalls that littered the mountain range created a soft background melody to the picturesque scene. Finally, the woman spoke, "That was a close call."

"Yes," the policeman said, "that was very close indeed, but our Father chose wisely in that one. He will certainly be useful in the coming times."

The three figures continued to stare at the horizon at the end of the valley and between the mountains just a moment longer before the policeman said, "Come, we must go and prepare for what is to come."

The two either side of the policeman turned and started walking, leaving the policeman to linger just a moment longer, before, he, too, turned and walked back. Within a few steps, he disappeared as well.

Printed in Great Britain
by Amazon